T0194314

THE *Memory* HIVE

A Novel

LAURA OTIS

THE MEMORY HIVE
A NOVEL

iUniverse books may be ordered through booksellers or by contacting:

iUniverse
1663 Liberty Drive
Bloomington, IN 47403
www.iuniverse.com
844-349-9409

ISBN: 978-1-6632-0773-9 (sc)
ISBN: 978-1-6632-0772-2 (e)

Library of Congress Control Number: 2020920963

Print information available on the last page.

iUniverse rev. date: 12/02/2020

Cells

lick. Sweet sound! My deadbolt slides into place. I turn the lock, fasten the chain, and I'm safe. Until I go out again, no one can hurt me.

"¡Puta!" Whore!

Oh no, there's Diego's voice. It's as if I'd swallowed him, and his snarl were tearing my insides.

How can people talk about "letting go"? There's nothing to release that's not part of me, no "me" that's unaltered by Diego. How would you let go of your own cells? What "me" exists apart from his voice?

Sometimes when I was lost in thought, Diego would tug at my elbow.

"What is it?" he demanded. "What are you thinking?"

I would have forgotten him as I listened to my mother's voice.

"I can always hear you coming," she used to say. "You have such a *heavy tread*."

Diego always knew when I was remembering, because my breathing changed. It got shallower, faster, he said, and sometimes I sighed on a high-pitched tone. It made him feel that I had left him, and he grabbed me to pull me back home.

If memory were a place where you went, it would be a beehive of cells. Every one of them would lead to more chambers, each with something that stings. Open and free, it would have no end, just infinite possibilities. But memory isn't a place where you go. Instead, it comes to you.

"¡Pónte recta!" Stand up straight!

I snap upright in a silent blue room. My fuzzy bears gaze with gentle sympathy. None of them said that. Where did that voice come from? When you've swallowed a voice, you can't purge it by writing. When you record it, you reproduce it, amplifying it by creating new copies.

"¡Zorra!" Bitch!

Diego's white face floats among the bears, distorted by the need to hurt. No cell walls can seal off my visions of Diego. Memory lives in me, through me.

Window Full of Shoes

I met Diego on a day of wildness. I just get wild sometimes. On that day, it happened because I wanted so badly to move. I had come to his town to read articles by Celia Rojas, who had explained heat and light to nineteenth-century women. His museum's library had the last remaining copies of her essays, and for days I had worked faithfully. I took notes at the archive and read in my shaded hotel room during the siesta hours between two and five. When the stores reopened and life returned to the streets, I rushed out for a few hours of pleasure. I stared at windows full of shoes as beautiful as candy, shoes that would have tasted like sugar if I'd licked the heels.

That day I felt hungry, and I was sick of fruit, nonfat yogurt, and dry brown bread eaten timidly in my room. On a back street, a smiling fat man on a sign advertised a menú del día: two hot dishes, dessert, and coffee for just 600 pesetas. I went in and ate it all, and when the waiter asked me if I wanted coffee, I took that too. Normally I don't drink coffee, since it makes me crazy, but on that day, I wanted it. After I drank the sweet, hot coffee, I refused to go back to my room.

Suddenly the three-hour curfew infuriated me. I had learned the hard way that during those forbidden hours, a woman can't walk on the street. If you do, you're immediately accosted by junkies, thin little men who follow you and won't go away. During the siesta, women serve food, wash dishes, watch soap operas, and talk with their families, all behind thick stone walls. If you venture out, you're unprotected. But where were we, Europe, or Afghanistan? Why couldn't I walk around in the middle of the afternoon?

Behind Diego's town was a rugged brown hill that cried out to be climbed. For days I had eyed it, longing to run up. Here I was, hovering in the shadows, when this green mound offered exactly the landscape that Celia Rojas had described. So that day I did it. Straight from the restaurant, I crossed a bridge over the river and asked a workman how to climb the hill. He told me there was a path, but it was dangerous, and I shouldn't go there. How could a hill be dangerous? What was up there, mine shafts? Snakes?

I was determined to do it, but I turned back quickly when the first path led to a Roma camp. The sight of me set off motion like that of quick, angry wasps. Luckily, I found another way up the hill, a deserted path with trembling red poppies and the scent of baking grass. Up and up I climbed, thighs pumping ecstatically, thrilled to have something to do at last. At the top, I spread my arms in a V and turned my face to the sky. Only buzzing insects scratched the silence, and the air in my nostrils was warm and sweet.

When I climbed back down, I went to the stores. For days I had been looking at clothes, conserving my money, but that day I dared to try something on. It was a stretchy little scrap of navy-blue cotton with a cool silver zipper between the breasts. When I saw myself in it, I couldn't believe I could look that sexy. I bought the top, and for the next two hours, I carried it around in a black plastic bag.

"Hey, you! Where are you from?"

The voice struck me as I studied a window full of shoes. I had heard Spanish words, but I hadn't listened, since I didn't think they were directed at me. The voice came from a taut, blond man with angular features and troubled blue eyes. I told him I was from New York, and we switched to Spanish. He and his dark-haired friend invited me for a drink, but out of habit I said no. You can't sit down with two guys you just met. But in the streets near the river, I ran into them again. A free water couldn't hurt, and it was a chance to speak Spanish, so I joined them at a wobbly table and talked of my love for Celia Rojas.

Diego, the blond one, walked back to town with me and persuaded me to come to a political rally—I never learned for what. Through all of it, he whispered in my ear, something no one had ever done to me before. The tickling puffs of air told me I shouldn't believe a word they were saying. They were all a bunch of bums, and he never voted. His family owned a sailboat, and his aunt worked at the library. With his connections, he would help me with my project.

My arousal arced in flashes, glowing as it circled in my womb. Most of the men I knew looked as though they had been poured into their clothes, but Diego had the best posture I had ever seen. He was tense, angry, snapping with energy. At the same time, I felt sorry for him. He was trying to impress me, but everything he offered came from a link to someone else. *Haven't you— haven't you ever* done *anything?* I wondered. But with a dead father and 23 percent unemployment, there wasn't much he could do. In his world, everything happened because of connections, and you impressed strangers by showing who you knew.

People said that Diego looked like my brother. We had the same blond eyebrows, hollow cheeks, and tight intensity. I had never known anyone who looked like me, and I took it as fate. Diego was my partner, my twin.

Soon the town accepted us as a couple. During the siesta we ate picnics in my room, with the window open to the air shaft and the radio playing. I discovered that Diego had dark moles pocking his body, so he wasn't exactly my twin.

"Eres guapísima," he told me, his eyes open with wonder. "You're beautiful. I can't believe you don't have a boyfriend."

For him, as for me, it had been a long time. "El calvo," he called himself, baldy. "Calvo," he had said to himself, "if this keeps up, you're going to get rusty."

On the weekend, he borrowed his sister's car, and we

Laura Otis

rode out to the green hills Celia Rojas had described. In the sweet air, I sang out loud. I taught Diego the bear song, which he tried to repeat:

The other day I met a bear

Out in the woods away up there.

The other *day* I met a bear

Scaddy waddy waddy doo

Out in the woods away up there.

But his favorite word was one he couldn't pronounce: Manhattan. Manhattan. Manhattan.

Under Diego's influence, I came home later and later. My body likes to rise with the sun and go to bed when it sets, but Spain comes alive in the dark. One night the sunscreen I had smeared on that morning ran into my eyes, so that tears streamed out of them and I was completely blind. Diego led me through the hotel restaurant, clutching a bunch of wildflowers from the hills.

"How sweet," I heard people saying. "They've had a lovers' quarrel."

Another night, in the plaza under a full moon, I told Diego all about Jim.

"I could kill him," he said. "He's married?"

It pleased me that he wanted to kill Jim.

That night junkies were blocking the hotel entrance, and Diego signaled the clerk to let us in a side door. A man with vacant eyes stood with a syringe bobbing in his arm. Diego explained that in the jubilation after Franco, a lot of kids had tried drugs and become addicted, people from his school, people he knew.

I felt terrified to meet his mother and sisters, but we got along well. They lived in a long, multiroom apartment that he called a "casa," a house. When Diego and I ate something, I said we should wash the dishes, but he told me the maid would do that. His mother was blonde and ferocious; his younger sister, spiritual and intense. I didn't like his older sister, María del Rosario, who smirked at me and made fun of my accent. But his mother looked me up and down and invited me to Rosario's wedding. I was shocked. My own sister's wedding had cost sixty dollars a plate. I guessed Diego's mother saw me the way he did: as a gift from God that had fallen to earth.

By the time Rosario married, I had moved to Madrid. From novelist Celia Rojas, I had moved on to the scientist Rafael Anza and was studying the ways he described neurons. I found a furnished apartment near a round plaza, a hot, dusty place where Chinese students lived. I asked the overbearing receptionist what sort of wedding present to buy, and she told me "un detalle," a detail. I chose a beautiful crystal pitcher from a department store. It cost over thirty dollars, a small fortune.

To reach Diego's town, I rode six hours on a train, which crawled bravely along mountain ledges in a battering storm. For the wedding I put on the best clothes I had, my new aqua suit from Paris and the matching slip-back shoes from Madrid. Diego looked me up and down and registered distaste.

"Te faltan medias," he said. You need stockings.

In the casa, all hell was breaking loose. Diego's brother had failed to pick up his suit from the cleaners, and everyone was screaming at everyone else. Only Rosario sat calmly in the white gown she had designed, smoking a cigarette like a Toulouse-Lautrec girl. My little pitcher stood like a shrub in a shining forest of crystal. She never acknowledged it or said thank you, and I'm not sure she knew it came from me.

Rosario's classic ceremony made me doubt the life I had led, in which family and religion played no part. A graceful white bouquet hung from each pew, and the priest read from Corinthians about love. Rosario and her husband cut their fluffy cake with an actual silver sword. One by one, each of Diego's cousins greeted us.

An older man beamed at our twin blondness. "We have seven children! You should marry soon!"

Once the music started, we danced until two. I bounced delightedly to a song about a farmer in love with his tractor. I felt sorry for Diego's mother when he refused to dance with her. He hated her for doling out his allowance each week.

When the dancing stopped, I was ready for bed, but at three the whole wedding moved to a bar. *Doesn't anyone want to have sex?* I wondered. I begged Diego to let me sleep, but he said that we couldn't leave. I went to the bathroom to untangle my matted hair, but he found me crying and dragged me back out. Despite his mother's and my efforts to stop him, he had gotten drunk on Cuba libres, a poison of rum and Coca-Cola.

At five he pulled me into a throbbing purple disco, but I rebelled to save my life.

"This is *hell*!" I wailed.

When we finally went to bed, he asked me to be his wife.

"Sea mi mujer," he begged. "Cásate conmigo."

He had to be up at seven to go to the first job he had found in eighteen months, a two-week stint as a receptionist at a trade fair. Without my violent urging, he would never have gone. I left the pantyhose I had borrowed from his mother in a damp, stinking knot on the floor.

When Diego finished with the fair, he came to live with me in Madrid, which at first I didn't like. I had made a nice home in the white studio apartment with bright ceramic plates and cleaning supplies from hole-in-the-wall shops. His mother had advanced him his salary, since the trade fair wouldn't pay him for weeks. Spain was like that, he explained: when you finally did find work, they wouldn't pay you.

Before Diego came, I had begun to feel like myself again, working in the library and exploring the city. I would lock myself in when the shops closed at eight and not emerge again until the next morning. But Diego stayed up all night and never rose until noon. I remember, in tears at 4:00 a.m., begging him to let me sleep.

Instead he shook me and yelled, "But look! Your favorite movie is on! ¡*Entre tinieblas*!"

Twisting in bed, we tore the thin cotton sheets to

shreds. Our feet turned black from the sooty floor. In a hot city where you keep the windows open, you have to mop the room each day—which we didn't do. We would wash our feet, but by the time we'd walked from the bathroom to the bed, they would be black again.

"¡Qué asco!" he exclaimed. How disgusting!

I felt as though I were turning into something dirty.

We ate squishy bread from the convenience store, since we never got out before the bakeries closed. At one, Diego would walk with me to the library, where I would find him waiting anxiously to pick me up at six. I hated myself for working so little but felt powerless to break the cycle. No one had wanted me like this for so long.

One day when I was dressing, he put his hand on my stomach and said, "¿Sabes una cosa?" You know what? "Quiero hacerte mamá."

I had never known a guy who wanted to have kids. To the men I knew in grad school, marriage and kids were a form of asphyxiation that lasted for life.

On the weekends, we took trips that I paid for. Once we went to Toledo, where I showed Diego the cathedral, the synagogue, and El Greco's *Burial of the Count of Orgaz*. Diego had stopped in the medieval city a few times but only to drink beer in bars. Proudly, I translated an English-speaking guide's explanation of El Greco's painting. I was getting pretty good at simultaneous translation.

Another weekend we took the train south to Mérida, the Roman city I had longed to see. Here, with the temperature over 110, the whole town lived at night. We went to a Shakespeare play in the Roman theater that ran from eleven until two. Next day, we had only an hour in the precious Roman museum, since it opened at nine and closed at one. Diego talked loudly about how someday, we would do this right. We would drive down in a big air-conditioned car and stay in a four-star hotel. In our tiny, oven-like room, we got almost no sleep at all.

In Madrid, I began to discover a strange thing about Diego. When he got upset, he would yell for hours. After the trip to Toledo, we came back late, and drug dealers had occupied the streets. Along Gran Vía, every three or four meters stood a tall African man selling drugs. Half running, Diego dragged me through the streets like a rag doll. I couldn't break his steel grip on my wrist. Any way we rushed, we found more statue-like dealers, and Diego's voice became a television turned up too loud.

"¡Joder!" Fuck! We've put ourselves in the very worst place!

Another time, a woman on a scooter skidded and fell with a sickening crack. She staggered up and talked dazedly in Portuguese, reeling from some kind of drug. She was bleeding, and I wanted to help her, but Diego yelled for me to stay back. Who knew what kinds of diseases she had? He raced through the streets shouting for an hour, repeating everything his friend Paco, a doctor, had said to do after an accident. If a woman was hysterical, you had to smack her across the face. After that, we fought most of the night.

I said he was making an excuse to hit women. You couldn't hit a person anytime, ever.

Yes, you could, cried Diego, if she was hysterical.

"¡Si me pegas, te dejo!" I spat. If you hit me, I'll leave you!

Diego inched forward on the bed. Suddenly I felt as if he were a grown-up and I were a little girl.

"Maybe I made a mistake in coming here," he said. "Maybe I should go back home."

My stomach churned, and the world revolved the way it always did when a man wanted to leave me. With every bit of force I had, I begged him not to go. Life had become unimaginable without Diego.

It was I, not he, who kept urging marriage. One day I took him to the American embassy and asked them how to get married. What kinds of papers and tests did you need? Diego got a sheepish, little-boy look on his face like a guy from a 1950s sitcom who says "Gee whiz." But I wanted to do it, and he wanted to do it. We talked about my job in New York and the wonderful life we would have.

The day before I left, Diego started yelling again. I was going home to find a place for us to live, and he would follow me a month later. Probably he feared I would change my mind and tell him not to come. I got crazy myself when I called home and tried to tell my sixty-three-year-old mother when I was coming. Demented and frightened, she couldn't take down a single digit of the flight information. She let the phone fall with a clunk as she groped for a pen, panting with fear that something had happened to her daughter. Meanwhile, the phone meter registered the excruciatingly expensive seconds, and Diego roared for me to hang up. I cried and screamed with terror when I learned that my sister would be in the house. Diego called me hysterical and didn't understand.

As I packed my bags, he yelled about the incompetence of women.

"Stop patronizing me!" I cried.

Then he discovered that my ticket had me leaving at nine, and my itinerary, at three.

"With this in my hand, I will sue them!" he shouted.

The night went on like this. In the morning, we staggered from the subway to Colón, where the bus would take me to the airport. That was the last I saw of Diego, angry, electric, and near tears, uncertain whether he would ever see Manhattan.

Jim

Jim and I first noticed each other while he was giving a talk on *Gravity's Rainbow*. In my indigo-blue blouse, I sat listening intently, feeling the intellectual, spiritual, and erotic pull. Later Jim told me that he wanted me right then, but what could he do? He had to talk about information, chaos, and hidden spots of order.

I approached him afterward, spoke to him about Pynchon, and asked him if he wanted to have lunch. In an echoey food court, over brown Chinese food, we talked about space, time, and writing. He came from a neighborhood where boys beat him up and no one ever went to college. He had escaped through the army, then studied computer science. Now he was earning a PhD, but his professors didn't like his interest in literature. Two hours disappeared without any sign of their passing, and in all that time he never mentioned a wife. Wife? Who had a wife? No computer science student I'd ever heard of. They didn't have girlfriends, let alone wives. I never looked at his hands, because his face was so fascinating. He seemed to radiate light.

Jim was six two, straight-backed and lean, with long legs and wiry arms. Physically, he didn't look like my type at all. I like short, stocky, black-haired guys with thick arms and eyes that burn with intelligence. Jim had an elongated face, with gray hair and musing, dark eyes.

In the midst of our talk, an unknown voice came out of me. I don't know how, or from where. I told him that the previous night at my motel, I had wanted to watch *Miami Vice*, but the picture kept tumbling. I wish there had been a scientist around to fix my TV set, I said. I actually told him that. It just came out of me, and he leaped for the bait.

"Can we fix it right now?" he asked. "Please, please can we?"

Then I realized what I had said. No, I told him. I didn't mean that. I blushed. I mean, you can't have sex with someone you just met three hours ago—can you?

"Oh, please let me fix your TV set!"

"No."

We settled for a kiss goodbye. At the entrance to an art museum, he pulled me to him, and my feet left the ground, since I'm a foot shorter than he is. It was like no kind of bonding I've felt before or since.

"Here, now, none o' that!" laughed an old guard, cheering us on.

That was the last I saw of Jim for six months. I wrote him and sent him a copy of my paper, and he sent me his, but the flatness of his writing surprised me. He seemed to be in another world, and after the letter with his paper, he didn't write back.

We next saw each other at a literature conference. I recognized his posture first, taut and perfect amidst round, slouching figures. When I saw his eyes on me, the room dissolved, and I could hardly breathe. I knew that something was going to happen, but we had to stand in a circle of people and talk about tenure requirements.

While I was speaking to a woman from New Zealand, I noticed rays of light reflected from his hand. A ring. He was wearing a ring. The dull gold looked like part of his finger, as though the two had grown together the way a tree expands around a cord on its trunk. I sank down into dark, wet horror like a water-skier whose line has been cut.

When we spoke, the people around us disappeared. Maybe they were still there, but I didn't sense them.

"You're married."

"Does that matter?"

We talked as though something irreversible had happened, although nothing had happened yet.

"Well, how do you think your wife would feel if …"

"She'd probably feel pretty bad."

It didn't stop him. He amazed me. I couldn't understand why he thought it was all right.

We decided to talk about it at the Dog Hill Diner.

"We'll have to sublimate," I said.

"I don't think that will be enough."

I held out for twenty-four hours, then invited him to the Run-Rite Inn. I've never been able to stand the claim that I'm withholding something from someone. I had catalyzed whatever was happening, and I must have wanted him even if I couldn't admit it consciously. The joy of being wanted vindicated my life. His desire was the force of gravity, a life-ordering pull.

That day was my birthday. I turned twenty-seven, and I learned that I was small. Five two, 105 pounds, perseverant and agile. I became a gymnast—he took me backwards, forwards, standing up, lying down, with my ankles on his shoulders. For hours we lay there, his fluids drying to a crust on my abdomen, talking about things we did in a day. Some days he cooked lentil soup, he said, and we talked about the best way to make it. He tested me on *Star Trek* trivia, and he told me what his wife looked like. His honesty hurt.

"Her breasts are bigger than yours" was the first thing he said.

He had no complaints, not a bad word to say about her, and it was clear he wanted her for life. He just wanted me too and saw no contradiction. I turned the thought over, considered it quietly.

Jim's friend drove me to the bus station in a rented white Cherokee. Jim sat in front, and I in back, and once he reached back to touch my hand. I gripped it, then pushed his fingers away. On the ride home, I watched raindrops creep across the bus windows as I rolled past wet orange hills. I couldn't call him, couldn't write to him, and I wouldn't see him for a year. He sent me a haunting poem about fluids and leaves.

The next year, Jim brought his wife to the conference. This was hell unimaginable. I wore my long hair up so that she couldn't chop it off, and I expected to see her as I turned each corner. In the end, hair played a crucial role in our meeting. My desire to be seen had vanquished my fear, and in a bathroom, I was brushing

Laura Otis

out my hair. A lady was admiring it—How long! How bright! How silky!—and just then, a woman who fit his description of his wife stepped out of a booth. With my head sideways, still brushing, I read her badge backwards in the mirror. It was her, my exact opposite. She wore a white shirt, a maroon jumper, and brown cowboy boots, and she was powdering her face with a giant brush. She had wavy, chin-length black hair, and her body exuded warm softness. Next to her, I was a tiny, taut demon of energy. I'll never forget the look of anguish on her face. It wasn't rage, just hurt. When I came out of the bathroom, Jim stood waiting. But not for me—he was waiting for her.

He sat down with me for a few minutes to tell me what was happening.

"I'm sorry I can't spend any time talking to you this year," he said. "My wife's here, and I've told her everything. Right after we got back. We do everything together. She saw it all right away."

So his emotions after that last meeting must have been as keen as mine. I respected his wife for wanting to keep him. He said that after he told her, he had experienced the worst time of his life.

"But I'm not sorry," he said. "I'm not sorry for anything we've done."

The next time I saw him (same meeting, next year), Jim was alone. His wife had stayed home with their newborn baby boy.

This was the crux, the most powerful time. He had promised her not to see me, and this time, he couldn't tell.

We both held back, but we couldn't resist the afternoon. We walked out into the city, resuming our conversation as though nothing had happened. Our bond was so intense, he knew my thoughts, and I could finish his sentences. Our bodies moved differently when we were together. Normally his gestures were uncertain, but around me he swaggered. His strides became long, his face ironic. Anytime we saw each other, his eyes brightened with mischievous irony, as though we were sharing a secret joke.

In the park where we walked, the air was clear and cold. Bright orange leaves dropped steadily, and a white city lay spread out below. He groped and pulled at me more roughly than I wanted. I felt nervous, since there were children playing nearby. As it grew darker, we kept walking, uncertain. He had promised not to have dinner with me, but we were growing hungry and cold. Usually a good navigator, I felt lost and bewildered and let him lead the way. We stopped in awe before an abandoned church, black and grassy with beckoning darkness. He wanted to explore it, but I said it was a shooting gallery—probably full of needles.

We ended up at the door of my tiny hotel, and I begged him to come in. He looked down at me with a half smile, hesitating for an eternity. In the frigid blackness, I couldn't read the energy in his dark eyes. Suddenly, he grasped me and pressed me to him until I thought my ribs would crack. As our breathing harmonized, his grip softened, and we stood together, yin and yang. I knew he would never come inside me again, but I've never felt closer to anyone.

Laura Otis

In the weeks after that, Jim's absence nearly drove me mad. In Boston, rain rotted the fallen leaves to fetid paste, which I mashed as I walked over redbrick sidewalks. I sent Jim a card, but he typed a few lines, asking me not to write to him. His wife picked up his mail at school, and she mustn't think I was obsessed with him. Obsessed? I read everything he had written over and over, as though it were in secret code. I listened to the Police's *Synchronicity* as I read and reread my diary entries about him. Saturdays, when I was done grading papers, I searched for cheap, sexy clothes and imagined him admiring me. Obsessed? Why do men think you're mentally defective if you feel?

A year and a half later, I walked into Diego's town in Spain. One night with the moon shining down in the plaza, I told him about Jim.

"Quiero matarlo," said Diego. A married man? And my heart belonged to him?

Yes, I said. It was Jim that I loved.

When Diego wanted to marry me, I saw it as a way to get clean. I was a free radical, a maverick thirty-one-year-old woman who wanted married men and was wanted in turn. If I were just removed from circulation, I could stop hurting people. I could stop endangering society. I liked the idea—marriage as maturity, a call to order.

So I said I would do it.

Only years later did I realize I had married someone with the same name in a different language.

Maintaining the Home

When I got home in mid-August, I had three weeks to buy a car, insure it, prepare three courses, find an apartment, and move into it, all before Diego arrived. I did everything, but I spent most of that time on something more important: cleaning my parents' house.

My parents had always been slobs, but as my mother grew crazier, the mess started looking like her mind. When I was eleven, I took over the cleaning, spending Saturdays straightening, dusting, and vacuuming and Sundays folding and ironing the wash. My mother, a teacher, graded papers all weekend, and my father did the laundry and laid out leftovers for lunch. My sister slept most of the day. Sometimes she came out of her room and snarled.

When I went away to college, the mess took over. I cleaned and organized on vacations, but that was never enough. Fascinated by my parents' chaos, I conducted experiments. One Christmas, I left a shoebox on a living room bookcase. When I came back at Easter, it was still there. The misplaced objects stuck like my sister, defiantly asserting their presence.

Weeks earlier in Madrid, when I'd heard my sister would be at my parents' house, I burst into desperate sobs.

"Take deep breaths! Take deep breaths!" bellowed Diego. He thought I was ridiculous. How could anyone be so afraid of spending a few weeks with her sister?

My sister—the epicenter of a human earthquake. At thirteen, she stopped going to school.

"You don't *have* to do anything," she told me.

The State filed a suit to have her removed from my parents' care, and they scrambled to find a private school, which expelled her. My mother, who hid my body under men's clothes, bought her a slinky black dress, which she drenched with pee on a drunken night. She ran away and got as far as Norfolk before learning the people she was running to didn't want her. In an argument, she shoved my mother back and raked the air threateningly with her claws. She spent weeks in a psychiatric ward, where she created a black-clad self-portrait blazing with intensity. She slashed her wrists, her face, and her chest with razor blades until I hid them in a Greek vase. My mother loved that gray vase with black figures, which she had bought at the World's Fair before she married. She never looked inside it, or she might have found steel leaves wrapped in paper to preserve their sharpness.

Once my sister tried to OD on my mother's blood pressure pills and told me, "I thought I was gonna *die*!"

My parents did nothing to stop her. To them, she was like the weather, something unfortunate that had struck them.

In her teens, she married a patronizing man who wanted to teach his wife. He helped her earn her GED and attend college, but he called her a leech, a lump, and a blob. She had never worked full-time, didn't have children, and rivaled my parents for household chaos. Often she slept through the days, then got up and paced around at night.

Periodically, she spoke of leaving her husband, so that my father would call me, trembling with fear. We knew that if she came home, shock waves of pain would shoot from her, knocking us off our feet. The last time she came, when my mother was fading, she lectured my mother on "maintaining the home."

"Why don't you wash your hair! You look like a street person!" she yelled.

She stormed out on foot and moved in with a friend who had a great mane of red hair. My father used to see them together at the mall, and he had to deal with her furious husband.

"She's not here," he told him each morning.

Her husband threatened and roared, and my father had to listen to his wrath. But incredibly, after a month, she went home. Her husband threatened to take her dogs to the pound, and that must have had some effect.

My sister used a different torture for each person, one that suited their personality. With me, it was to convince me that she knew about life and I didn't. In the worldview she spread, she had wisdom; and I, SAT scores. She knew about people; and I, about characters. In anything that happened outside a classroom, I ranked in the bottom 5th percentile. As I showed her my ring, she looked with patronizing approval, and she offered wedding tips from magazines. In glowing summer twilight, I told her I wanted to marry because I had so much in my life, I wanted to share it. She smiled as though she were welcoming me to a higher moral order.

As it turned out, her presence didn't do much harm, because she slept most of the time. By spending her days unconscious, she avoided dealing with my mother, who is diurnal. I saw her only very late at night, at the ends of my nineteen-hour cleaning days.

I fell into a veritable cleaning frenzy. I became a Tasmanian devil desperate for order. Every horizontal surface in that house was covered with six inches of rubble: unopened mail, newspapers, uncapped lipsticks, notepads, matzahs, pieces of string. My mother's old dittoes from school nuzzled used napkins, dog leashes, and plastic bags of coins. Dead plants stiffened on each windowsill, and fruit was rotting on the kitchen counters. In the shower I found mushrooms sprouting. Bits of crystallized chicken dotted the Persian rug. It disgusted and horrified me that my father lived this way, but he shrugged his shoulders and laughed.

As a madwoman's keeper, he had to set priorities, and cleaning the house wasn't one of them. He wanted to give my mother some pleasure in her last years, so he took her to the beach, to restaurants, sometimes to concerts.

He went to work each day because it was his only contact with normal people, and as she deteriorated, he had less time to maintain the home. Anytime he turned his attention from my mother, she stormed, stomped, and screamed. She called for help when he washed the dishes, and she raged when he tried to read the mail. Once when he went to the bathroom, she ran out and got lost. Gradually, he had given up doing anything. He couldn't hire a cleaning lady, since no one could clean until the rubble was cleared. The debris covered every table and bookcase and also much of the floor.

Every cabinet was filled to capacity so that if you opened it, food fell in your face. My mother complained that she couldn't find things, and my father's solution was to "saturate the house": to buy so many flashlights, jars of pumpkin pie spice, and Salmon Frost lipsticks that eventually you had to find some by sheer odds.

The yard paralleled the house in its growth. Originally, the plan had been good. Gardens softened the edges of a bright green lawn. But as the border garden shrubs became trees, my mother grew dissatisfied. She wanted to plant blue hydrangeas, and to make space for them, she ordered my father to dig holes in the dense green grass. The border garden became an impenetrable forest, and the oil company threatened to stop delivering if we didn't trim the bushes back. A friend in a wheelchair became irate when branches whacked his face as he rolled up the front walk. With violent fierceness, my mother forbade my father to cut back any living thing. My father never dared to disobey.

In the house, the rubble that most offended me was the cascade on the piano: junk mail, old Christmas cards, boxes of dried-out pens.

"This is a musical instrument!" I cried.

The saddest thing was, no one could play. I was the one with the ear, inherited from my father's mother, the organist. But for perverse reasons, I wouldn't practice. My mother wrung her hands and radiated all the guilt she could muster, but the systematic energy I applied to everything else had never gone to that. If I wanted to play a piece, I would pick it out by ear, but I never learned to play properly. The debris suffocating that poor piano reminded me of all our failures.

With my fake diamond ring sliding up and down my finger, I cleaned every day from 6:00 a.m. until 1:00 a.m. I rolled up $300 in loose change. I attacked cabinets where ancient cans of food had ballooned and burst. I picked pennies off of drawer bottoms where they had fused with melted hard candy. I fought sloth, incompetence, and waste like a gladiator with a dull sword.

"Do you really have to do that?" asked my father sadly, seeing me roll pennies at 1:00 a.m.

No, I thought, *YOU really have to do this*, but I didn't say anything.

My father was devastated by the news I wanted to marry. His parents had divorced after decades of screaming fights. His oldest sister, an alcoholic, had run away from home at fifteen and married several times. The second oldest followed soon after. The saddest case was that of his youngest sister, the butch one who could fix machines. His two older sisters taunted her mercilessly because she didn't smoke or wear makeup. No man will ever want you, they jeered. So she married a guy who beat her up regularly, and she didn't divorce him for twenty years. Gradually she accumulated enough material to put him in jail for life: corrupt business practices as well as cruel abuse. But one night someone broke into the lawyer's office, and all the files disappeared. She had to start from scratch and didn't do well in the settlement. Soon after that, she died of lung cancer from the cigarettes her sisters convinced her to smoke.

When my father heard I was marrying a smoker, it hit him like a mortal blow. As he saw it, I was killing myself, since to both my parents, marriage meant suicide. "When you marry, your life is over," he used to tell me. "When you have children, your life is *really* over." He believed this not just because of his mother's and sisters' misery but because my mother had convinced him he had killed her life by marrying her. My sister and I were two silver bolts holding her coffin shut.

In an extraordinary act of assertiveness, he looked me in the eyes, shook his head, and begged me, "Don't do it."

I didn't respect his warning, because he had always advised me not to do anything. "Don't try anything; you might get hurt" seemed to be the motto of his life. But this time he was right. One of the worst things about marrying Diego was how much I hurt my father.

Twenty

Diego was the twentieth man I had slept with. Let's see. There was

1) Joe

2) Carlos

3) Nick

4) Lin

5) Jia

6) Josh

7) Dave

8) Rob

9) Matteo

10) Johnny

11) Todd

12) Horacio

13) Martin

14) Roddy

15) Bruno

16) Girish

17) Jacob

18) Didi

19) Jim

and then 20) Diego

Maybe I shouldn't have told Diego. It might not

have been the best plan. I wanted to restart at year zero, confess everything, and in doing so somehow erase it. But it didn't work. Diego didn't like it. He said that he should go around wearing a T-shirt that said "20."

In one of film's most subversive moments, Carrie in *Four Weddings and a Funeral* matter-of-factly lists her previous thirty-two lovers to Charles, who has just become thirty-three. Women aren't supposed to do that. Actually, *people* aren't supposed to do it, but it would be wrong to think that those of us who do it, do it for power.

Why so many? In my case, I had made the same mistake each time. I wanted a boyfriend, not a list. I couldn't believe that one person could come inside of another without liking her, wanting to spend time with her, hoping to know her better. But they rarely did. If I could say they were shallow and dumped me because I was fat, I would feel better, but the truth was worse. They liked my looks fine; it was my soul they didn't want. By the time I met Diego, I had decided that a man wants to have sex with a woman and then kill her afterward so she can't ever bother him again. With some exceptions, men regarded my presence as a penance to be paid for a few quick flashes of pleasure.

Once I had a friend who stayed for two years with a man who humiliated her daily. When I asked her why she did it, she said it was because he wasn't ashamed to be seen with her. Her last boyfriend, a professor, had dropped her blocks away from work each day so that no one could see them walk in together. Diego *wanted* the world to know that I was his, and for me, that was glorious.

Diego never gave me a list of his own, just complained about a few who were especially bad. But my list fertilized his vine-like fears. He always suspected I was on the lookout for number twenty-one.

My Way

I took pride in the place I found for Diego and me to live: the upper half of a brown house in a vast development. The owner, Jeff, taught gym at a nearby school in a neighborhood where I wouldn't have dared walk. When he secured this job, his father, a contractor, helped him buy the house and outfit the top floor so that the rent would cover his mortgage payment. I respected Jeff for teaching sports to kids and managing his living situation so intelligently.

I had a tough time even visiting Jeff's apartment. At $670 a month, he had priced it so low that he received dozens of calls each day. He let me come look at it because I was a professor, and a professor wouldn't trash the place. I seemed respectable and had both parents with me, since my mother could still pass for human back then. She liked Jeff's muscles and hoped that I would forget Diego and marry him instead. While we were there, at least seven more prospective renters called, so I felt triumphant when Jeff picked me. He wanted only one person and didn't like the sound of a Spanish husband, but the word *professor* worked wonders.

You entered our apartment by walking around back, up a wooden staircase and onto a deck. When you pulled open the sliding glass door, you stepped into a foamy sea of pale-blue carpet, then into a small kitchen with black linoleum and a humming refrigerator. If you turned left, you reached the tight waist of the place, where the original staircase led up from below. At the head of the sealed-off stairs was a little bathroom, then finally a bedroom with the same powder-blue carpet. For me alone, it would have been perfect, since there was one of everything. I had never lived with a man for more than a few months, and I couldn't picture the place with two. I imagined twice one, two of me, and that seemed as though it would work.

One strong moving man delivered my furniture, and I arranged each piece with the greatest joy. Into the living room went my pink futon, my thirty-nine-dollar bookcase, my two-drawer file cabinet that served as an end table, and the coffee table I had finished with my own hands. Into the kitchen went my knives with pink plastic handles and my eight-dollar set of Brazilian dishes, creamy white with sky-blue rings. Into the bedroom went my mattress and box spring, sawed in half to make a tight corner in a Boston staircase. At the home store I bought cinder blocks for my bookshelves. I took the greatest pleasure in placing each item to best advantage. I had screwed together or varnished almost all the furniture, and I knew where I had bought everything and how much it had cost.

In the days before Diego arrived, money colonized my mind. I wondered how we were going to live. After taxes, I would earn about $1,600 a month. Rent was

$670. Diego would need warm clothes for winter, and we would have to eat. Car payments were $200, and car insurance was $160. Just after signing the lease for Jeff's apartment, I had bought Nadia, a slim, elegant Nissan Sentra. I had named her Nadia after Nadia Comaneci, the brave, solemn-eyed Romanian gymnast. When Nadia won her first perfect ten in 1976, I had jumped to my feet and applauded, alone in my room. Since my car was a Nissan, she needed an *N* name, and I hoped she could fly like Nadia.

Before Diego landed, I sometimes talked with Jeff, who did some rather odd things. He had been looking for someone to fix our phone, and once when we were out on an errand together, he spotted a phone truck and stopped to ask the driver to repair our phone right then. By stopping, he completely blocked the roadway, so that the hindquarters of the car behind him jutted out into a rushing street.

"Hey, BUDDY!" roared the trapped man behind us. "Yer blockin' the friggin' road! I'm out in the middle of the friggin' road here!"

I begged Jeff to drive on, since the repairman couldn't abandon his schedule to fix our phone.

"Take it easy!" he yelled to the poor man behind him, who quieted when he saw Jeff's size.

A few days later, Jeff rapped on the sliding glass door. He was going to an active singles weekend in the Catskills, but he had missed the last train that would get him to the pickup point on time. Could I drive him into Manhattan? I had owned Nadia for three days, and

I had grown up scared of the city. Driving to Manhattan was something you didn't do. But Jeff was my landlord. What could I say?

With white, rigid fingers, I drove us through the tunnel into the city, with Jeff coaching and encouraging me.

"Driving in New York, you gotta be aggressive," he urged.

I just wanted to get out alive. I left a smiling, grateful Jeff on an Upper East Side corner, then found the 59th Street Bridge. Once I had crossed it, I recognized nothing but Queens Boulevard. No expressway, no parkway, just lights, potholes, and thousands of careening cars. I knew that if I kept heading east, I couldn't go wrong, so that's what I did. When I hit the Cross Island Parkway, I turned south, and before I knew it, I was back home. Nadia's airbag remained safely wadded inside her gray steering wheel.

I soon learned that our living space was conjoined with Jeff's. The house had been designed for a single family, and despite the upstairs kitchen his father's men had built, the house had just one of everything. Our phone lines crossed, and three workmen had to come before we stopped receiving Jeff's calls. There was one driveway, one mailbox, one washing machine—all his— and worst of all, we heard everything in his apartment.

When I was growing up, my mother cursed our cheap walls, half-inch layers of Sheetrock tacked to a wooden frame. My sister and I laughed when our parents discussed us downstairs.

"Should we punish the child?"

"I don't know. What do you think?"

In Jeff's house, when he listened to music, we couldn't hear our TV, and he played music late into the night. He worked as a DJ at a local station, and his favorite singer was Frank Sinatra. I loved *Guys and Dolls* and had nothing against Frank, but it was different when Frank's voice shook the floor. For Christmas, Jeff got a karaoke machine, and then he sang along with Frank—a quarter tone flat.

Diego was astounded, then enraged. He had grown up in a solid apartment where no noise penetrated from the outside. The trouble with American houses, he declared, was that they were made of fucking wood, *de puta madera*. He wanted to go down and yell at Jeff. About once a week, Frank crooned, Jeff yodeled, and Diego screamed, all at a hundred decibels. I would cry, my heart pounding, my chest burning, and beg Diego not to start trouble. The guy downstairs was our landlord. Almost always, I convinced Diego to let me call Jeff instead, and I asked him politely to turn down the music. He always did, and he said he was sorry, but a week later he and Frank would be back.

Sometimes it got so bad that I cried and screamed and pounded the wall with my fists. Once he woke us up at one thirty in the morning, singing.

"I did it *myyyyyyyy* way!"

That time I was less polite.

Diego told me patronizingly that I had made a mistake. All his friends at Educational Services said their worst living experiences had been with the landlord downstairs. Since college, I had always lived this way, but back then, the landlord had been an old lady whose kids had moved out. It helped to have her lurking below, since any plumbing or electrical crisis affected her as much as it did me. In Boston, when my old landlord suddenly died, his nephew had blasted "I Will Always Love You" at 3:30 a.m. Still, I felt a deep inner rage at being told I had managed things badly. Diego didn't compliment me on finding a pretty, green neighborhood or an unbelievably low rent.

I agreed with him, though, that we couldn't go on like this. When our lease ended, we would have to move out. So after a year, we left Jeff and Frank. Jeff remained friendly to the end, wondering why we didn't stay.

Arrival

I met Diego at the airport with a sunburst of yellow flowers. After one last day of cleaning, I revved up Nadia and drove to the florist at our development's portal. I had hardly ever bought flowers before, but people waiting at airports often clutched brilliant bouquets. Hardly anyone had ever met me at an airport, and I wanted to do for Diego what I wished people would do for me.

For an hour and a half, I scanned the human flow at the international arrivals terminal.

"Where are you coming from? Where did you just come from?" I asked everyone breathlessly.

People had flown in from Seoul, Frankfurt, London, Tel Aviv, everywhere in the world but Madrid. I began to doubt that I would ever find a traveler from Spain. When Diego did appear, he was as overwrought as I.

"Welcome to America," I said.

I handed him the flowers, but he didn't notice them. Instead he focused on the rippling six-lane curves of the Southern Parkway. The scale of the place overwhelmed him, as though someone had given him a drug his nervous system couldn't handle. In his Spanish town he had postured and bragged. Here he sat amazed, with enormous eyes.

Diego didn't want the barbecued chicken, baked potato, corn bread, and apple pie I had cooked, but he tasted the all-American meal to please me. Although it was September, he told me he was cold, and he shivered and shook as though he had a fever. Anxious to help him, I pulled out the warmest clothes I had, the ones I had worn to bed when my Boston attic was as cold as the air outside. I helped him into a white woolen cap and an ill-smelling sweater from Tibet and pulled the blankets up to his chin. He lay there like a baby, whimpering, "It's cold. It's so cold." I felt a slow-spreading puddle of disappointment.

The Yellow Crust

After Diego had been in the apartment a few days, a yellow-brown crust appeared on the toilet. It spread along the white rim like a rash, plainly visible since he didn't lower the seat. In the past when I had lived with guys, I had never noticed this mustard-yellow growth. With repulsion, I realized what it must be.

I cleaned the toilet with a special yellow sponge. It relieved me to see the creamy white curves, but next day, the yellow crust was back. To hold it in check, I had to kneel each day, wiping, inspecting, decontaminating. When I lived alone, I had scrubbed it once a month.

Curious, I asked my father about it. Supposedly men and women waged wars over lowering the toilet seat, but in our house, I had never found it up. My father said he always sat down to pee. He had been tamed early, the only man in a house with a mother and three sisters. His father, who liked to spend time with his girlfriend, must not have stayed home long enough to pee.

When I confronted Diego, he laughed about the yellow stains. His family employed a live-in maid, and he hadn't cleaned a toilet in his life. At first, he made an effort and smeared the yellow drops with a dry, hard sponge. He didn't know that a sponge had to be wet to work, or that he needed to use Lysol. Having lived for thirty years with a maid, he couldn't believe he had to wipe his own pee.

So I kept on cleaning. If I hadn't, the poor, creamy toilet would have choked under the mustard crust. Each day as I knelt down to clean the rim, I thought about the stolen minutes. With every stroke of the sponge, my anger grew.

The Wedding

I wanted to marry Diego. The whole business was my idea. People have told me I was duped by a con man, but I wanted to marry him. I talked him into it.

In Madrid, I told Diego of my freshman-year roommate, who called my relationship with Carlos a cop-out when I wouldn't marry him at twenty-one.

"You don't marry your boyfriend when you're twenty-one!" I exclaimed.

"But you do when you're thirty-one?" he snapped.

There he had me, and I thought about my friend Steve, who had broken up with a woman when she wanted to marry him. He said he didn't think she loved him for himself; he'd just fallen in the path of her marriage train.

For good reason, Diego suspected my motives. I was about to turn thirty-two and wanted to try marriage. I had never met a man who wanted to marry a woman, let alone me. I didn't have too much trouble convincing Diego. In Madrid, I led him to the American embassy.

"How do we get married?" I asked.

While cleaning my parents' house, finding our apartment, moving in, buying Nadia, insuring her, and preparing my classes, I looked for a justice of the peace.

We applied for our license in the nearest big town, but I wanted to marry in a place where I knew someone, and my only friends lived in the town where I went to grad school. Diego didn't care where we got married; to him, it was all an adventure. So for fifty dollars, I booked Justice Joseph Jones.

When Diego arrived in New York with two suitcases, one of them contained his marriage clothes: a beautiful, expensive navy-blue suit and shiny black shoes. I felt ashamed of what I was going to wear: the cheap, sexy brown suit I'd bought at the conference where I'd met Jim's wife.

"You wore a *brown suit*?" asked my sister, outraged that I had left her out. Her wedding had been a sticky, purple horror that cost $6,000, and I vowed not to create anything like that.

Diego and I drove off elated, laughing as the darkness fell. On the winding, pitch-black roads, frustrated locals tried to pass us, and Diego yelled that I was driving wrong. To let someone pass you, he shouted, you had to turn on the right-hand direction signal and pull to the side. I had never heard of such a thing. He seemed not to grasp the concept of fifty-five miles an hour, even when I told him how much a ticket cost. He would teach me how to drive! You had to find a guy speeding, "un liebre," a hare, then run along behind him. We rocketed together through the inky night.

Diego and I stayed at my friends' house, since it was parents' weekend at the university, and there wasn't a room for fifty miles. Early Saturday morning, we met

Justice Jones at an overlook beside a waterfall, where he'd suggested we do the deed.

Justice Jones had been right about the beauty of the place. In early October, the leaves shone yellow and orange, glinting in the black water below gray cliffs.

"Oh, how lovely! A couple's getting married!" said a woman as Justice Jones's voice boomed across the gorge.

We all felt nervous in our own ways. My friends thought I was committing suicide. Diego sweated because he couldn't understand the service. He had practiced saying "I do," but Justice Jones used an old-fashioned ceremony where you have to say, "I will." I trembled with guilt whose causes eluded me. I felt as though I were committing fraud. I had planned the wedding with the same frantic determination with which I do everything, but I sensed that I was doing something wrong.

Justice Jones made us swear we were marrying soberly, and with all due forethought. I wondered how many people married drunk. We had to plight our troth, and I considered what that might mean. I pictured someone in an awful plight drinking from a trough, but I didn't think that was it.

On the sunny day glowing with orange leaves, we wandered the trail beside the gorge. For brunch, we ate at a hamburger joint that served onion rings in baskets lined with red-and-white napkins. We watched a nerd game show on PBS while Marjorie, Ted, and Françoise made a special dinner with champagne.

For the first time in my life, I tasted a sip of

champagne. I regard alcohol as poison and won't drink the stuff. Pain has always kept me from swallowing carbonated drinks, which prick my tongue like the forks of a thousand devils. But with fear I realized I could drink this bitter froth. I didn't take a second sip, but Françoise did and laughed as the bubbles invaded her nose. Even after we went upstairs to consummate the marriage, we heard Françoise and the others laughing. We had almost as much fun as at Marjorie's wedding, when we'd roller-skated along the lakefront.

In the upstairs room, Diego told me that he loved me and that I was a gift from God. I was the best thing that had ever happened to him, and I said that I loved him too. The world faded to darkness as it does in movies, stirred only by giggles from below.

For breakfast, we went to a diner, and there the mood changed. Françoise had learned that her father and stepmother were splitting, and her avalanche of words buried the meal. Diego listened wide-eyed as she told of the divorce and her feelings of anger and betrayal. It bothered me that she dominated our last hours together. After all, what was the big deal? Her hippie parents had been divorced before. But Diego was shocked. Did such things often happen here? Marriage meant something different to him than it did to me. In my eyes, it was a temporary contract, a reversible experiment.

We left right after breakfast, since I had to teach at nine on Monday. All the way home, Diego drove eighty-five miles an hour. This time a policeman stopped us, and I begged Diego to let me talk. As it turned out, I didn't have to.

On the rear window, with soap, my friends had written "Just Married."

"Did you two just get married?" the policeman asked.

Even with his sunglasses, I could feel his eyes glow. I explained that Diego was from Spain, and that they didn't have speed limits.

"Well, tell him that in *Pennsylvania*, we drive sixty-five!" shouted the cop, trying to make his voice loud enough for Diego to understand.

He didn't give us a ticket, just told us to slow down. He congratulated us on getting married.

The Hammer

B eing married to Diego was like living in a metal trash can on which someone was hammering. His voice bored into my head like a metal proboscis. There was no rest, no peace, no escape from the noise. I had dreamed of a husband who would listen to me, but in our two years together, I barely got in a word. Every day Diego would pound me, always in a particular rhythm:

Ba da DA da da DA da da DA da da DA da!

"Sí, oso, sí," I gasped.

Oso, bear, that was our name for each other. I was osito, the little bear, and he was el oso grande. Neither one of us liked my first name, Cara, which in Spanish means "expensive."

Ba da DA da da DA da da DA da da Da da!

"Sí, oso, sí—"

From the time I could talk, I had been told not to make noise.

"Modulate your *voice*," said my mother. With cupped hands, she covered her ears and assumed a pained expression.

Only ill-bred people raised their voices. Animals roared to gain attention; human beings should use their intelligence. Ridicule sculpts behavior with a cruel hand, and to this day I can't shout. When I got mugged and a stranger's fist slammed my face, my scream stayed trapped in my throat.

My mother didn't have to work hard to train me. To me, noise has always meant pain. When I was little, I cried when people played the piano too loudly. If I heard a firecracker, I screamed and jumped. In Paris on Bastille Day, when I couldn't escape the blasts, I cried and shook uncontrollably. People have always told me not to fear noise, but fear has nothing to do with it. A loud noise hits me like a blow in the face, and I react as though I've been struck.

At Jones Beach, a long tunnel leads from Lot 3 to the boardwalk, and in it, young people test their voices. As their screams tore into me, I used to hold my ears and cry.

"They should be killed!" I wailed to my mother. "They should all be killed!"

My father, whose voice can barely be heard, said, "Diego has a very loud voice. It makes you want to do what he wants just to make him go away."

I decided that Diego talked so loudly because no one ever listened to him. When I asked him about this, he cried, and he said it was true. I begged him to stop yelling and covered my ears as my mother had, but it never had any effect. He believed that the bear who roared the loudest ruled the woods.

Funny, I barely remember a thing that Diego said when he hammered. He shouted about politics, money, morals, and people who'd wronged him and how he would avenge himself. The volume would jolt my attention for a moment, but the contents never entered long-term memory. All I remember is:

Ba da DA da da DA da da DA da da DA da!

"Stop it! You're like a hammer!" I cried.

Diego looked stricken. "That's what they told me in Spain too," he said.

After a while, when the pounding started, I withdrew to a world of frozen disgust. I believed that people who made that much noise should be killed.

Sancho Panza

I have always loved the sound of Spanish. When I speak it, I feel lithe and powerful. New York English slops around like a mouthful of bad food. Spanish words strike the ear taut, tight and clean: Oye, Mari, mira, ¿te has mirado en el espejo?

To learn Spanish, I had to brave the sulfurous guilt in which my mother tried to bury me. In seventh grade, I could choose which language to learn, and she said I should take French, the language of educated people. Spanish was the language of the uneducated: fat women who gobbled like turkeys on the subway. About Puerto Ricans she had plenty to say. They had as many babies as they wanted and expected other people to pay for them. They ate up half the money her father had killed himself earning—just look at how fat they all were. We should just *sink* the whole continent of South America. Spanish speakers had contributed nothing to the world, no literature, no culture, no art. And now I wanted to learn their language? What would I do with it? Stubbornly, perversely, I signed up for Spanish. I wanted to talk with the people on the subway. They seemed to have so much to say.

I worked so hard at Spanish that, in high school,

I won a trip to Mexico in a county contest. In college, I took advanced poetry classes, hung out with Puerto Rican students, and stayed for two years with Carlos, my Argentinian boyfriend. I even persuaded my mother to extend our family trip from France to the wildness of Spain. When she was there, a stomach virus floored her for a week, the result of Spanish filth. In sympathy, my father got sick too, and I spent most of the trip peeling guys off my sister. My mother never stopped talking about Spain, a land of utter depravity.

My passion for Spanish eventually led me to Diego's town. He claimed my Spanish was awful at first and that he had taught me everything I knew. The Puerto Rican students had said that if they couldn't see me (since I look like Heidi), they would have sworn I was from Argentina. Until I met Diego, no one had ever found fault with my Spanish.

One day in Madrid I asked for bread at a bakery, and the woman didn't understand me at first.

"¡Lo dijiste FATAL!" yelled Diego. You said it INCREDIBLY badly! He imitated the way he claimed my voice sounded: breathy, airy, and dumb. I got angry, and he said that I should learn to laugh at myself. It amazed me that he thought you could treat someone this way and then still live with her afterward.

Diego and I functioned almost entirely in Spanish. His English, which I never criticized, was abysmal. His teachers had beaten the grammar into him, but not the rhythm or the sound. What he had absorbed washing dishes in London proved counterproductive in New York. He learned our language against his will, since he considered it an outrage that he should have to learn English at all. He absorbed my language slowly because he hated it, and he bragged to everyone that his American wife spoke Spanish. Only at his angriest did he use English words. He meant to frighten and humiliate me, but they came out so stilted that the most terrifying moments became absurdly funny.

In English, Diego made Sancho Panza mistakes, slips that revealed the fault lines in a flawed system. He had learned about New York from *The Bonfire of the Vanities*, and he wanted to know all the ethnic names, from the euphemisms to the most ugly. He confused *WASPs* with *wops* until I begged him not to say either word. At the supermarket, he mixed up *kosher* and *coleslaw*. I knew one professor named Barry and another named Bernie, and he called them both Barney, like Fred Flintstone's pal.

Sometimes I felt sorry for Diego. During his road test, the instructor yelled, "Pull over! Pull over!" but Diego kept driving. He knew about *pull*, and he understood *over*, but who would have guessed that together those words meant drive to the side and stop the car? I felt sorrier for the road test instructor, who must have feared he was out with a maniac. I wondered how long it took him to realize that Diego didn't understand.

At the movies, Diego expected a simultaneous translation of United Nations quality. If I didn't provide one, he fumed with rage, giving no thought to the people around us. "What's happening? What's happening?" he demanded during *The Pelican Brief.* I told him I didn't know, since I couldn't understand the plot. The people sitting near us wanted us dead. On Long Island, couples often helped each other at movies, since so many of us were immigrants. I respected the murmuring old couples, in which whoever spoke better English would tell the other what was happening. But no one expected that two young blonds were confabulating in the same way. Furiously, Diego stalked out of *The Pelican Brief,* unable to believe I couldn't follow the plot. I was being lazy and spiteful, withholding the help he needed.

Diego never accepted that I didn't know or that my information was incomplete. Once he asked me what "to ask" meant.

"Preguntar," I answered without hesitation.

As we drove east on the Holland Turnpike, he began to shout with rage. "To ask" could also mean "pedir," to ask for, but I hadn't told him that. In Spanish, "to ask" and "to ask for" are two different verbs, and I'd forgotten to say what "ask" could mean when combined with a preposition. What the hell kind of professor was I, who couldn't even say what "to ask" meant? Obviously, I didn't care about him.

La Migra

M y father told everyone I had made a green card marriage. I begged him to stop saying this, or La Migra would arrest me. I didn't marry Diego so that he could get a green card. I married him to share my life with him. If we hadn't married, he couldn't have studied or worked, and our relationship would have had no chance.

Earning a green card is no easy matter, even if you do everything right. Once we were legally married, we approached La Migra to get the forms. There were reams of them, including health certificates to be signed by an approved doctor. One simpler form caught my attention: a paper promising that I would support Diego financially for three years. With misgivings, I signed the form, and the word *responsibility* floated in my brain like a smoky menace.

"El papeleo," the paper attack, Diego called his quest for legal status. That first fall became a scavenger hunt in which La Migra consumed most of my time, energy, and money. If I called with a question, they shunted me into an automated labyrinth where I wandered half an hour before hearing a human voice. One morning I desperately needed to grade papers, and they cut me off after twenty-five minutes on hold. I cried and screamed and pounded the blue carpet, but it was useless. I had to call back and lose another half hour.

Still, I respected La Migra. We couldn't let just anyone into the country. Diego and I headed nervously to our first appointment in a huge, gray Manhattan beehive. The official asked to see pictures of us together, but she didn't test us with *Newlywed Game* questions. Diego marveled at the enormity of the place: the two-hour line snaking through the skyscraper; the kiosk industry thriving in its shadows.

Next came a trip to the Social Security building to apply for Diego's work permit. An old woman was trying frantically to talk to officials who couldn't understand her Spanish. Diego nudged me on the shoulder to translate, and I felt a thrill of pride. He had always mocked my Spanish, but he must have thought I was good enough to help the desperate lady.

In the final step to obtain his green card, Diego braved La Migra alone. He came home marveling at his peers.

"¡Toda la negrada!" he exclaimed. The whole black wave.

He had just spent three hours in a waiting room where he had felt very white. To La Migra, he was just the same as any Ghanaian or Pakistani who had married an American woman. They suspected him and wanted proof that he wasn't parasitizing the country. I began to develop a secret liking for La Migra.

Matasanos

L a Migra made each applicant for a green card visit an approved doctor. We read through their list and chose one in Richmond City. The demand seemed reasonable enough; you don't want people running around with untreated diseases. But Diego felt insulted. The doctor was sure to be a matasanos, a kill-the-healthy.

Matasanos's office looked authentic. It had plants, magazines, and lots of Spanish-speaking kids. The little doctor had made La Migra's list because he spoke Spanish, although with a terrible gringo accent. He had learned Spanish in Mexico, where he had studied medicine. At this I became more nervous than Diego and started looking toward the door.

La Migra wanted a blood test and a chest x-ray. Of all the diseases they could have sought, they were looking for tuberculosis. Had nothing changed in a hundred years? If they had tested for AIDS, I would have understood. But why scan Diego's blood and lungs for a disease that had almost disappeared?

Diego tested positive for TB. On our second visit, Matasanos told him in gringo Spanish that he would have to undergo a three-month treatment. He might have caught the disease when someone coughed on him. Diego reacted as though he'd been told he had lice.

"¡No! ¡No! ¡Díle que no!" he yelled.

People with liver problems couldn't take the TB medicine, and Diego had an altered enzyme level. By drinking, he had already half killed his fine, filtering liver. "My traitorous liver," he used to call it when it failed to remove the poison fast enough.

"¿Beber?" asked the doctor, bringing his thumb to his lips in a gesture that suggested both drinking and nursing.

Diego had tested positive because in Spain, kids are inoculated against tuberculosis. His immune system had seen the bacteria—but dead, so that he could form antibodies against them. He called his friend Paco, a doctor, and they shouted at each other for half an hour until Diego understood.

But how could we make Matasanos believe us? How could we convince La Migra? On our way home from the office, Diego cried with rage and fear.

"I can't live in this fucking country! This country has nothing for me!"

But he didn't complain when La Migra passed him, because his chest x-ray was clear.

Boston

In October, it came time for the literature conference. Diego or no Diego, we convened each year, and it sobered me to think how much my life had changed since last fall. At the last meeting, Jim had carried his baby on his back, and he, his wife, and his son had been received as a literature-loving family. Meanwhile, I had danced with a jokester in movements so sexy I surprised myself. This year the meeting would be held in Boston, and we decided to drive up.

We bounced with excitement over our first trip out of town. Diego drove us up I-95 in a gray streak, and we parked Nadia in the bowels of a chic hotel.

Diego's presence utterly changed the meeting. Before him, the conference had crackled with eroticism, brilliant ideas, bodies vibrating with intelligence. For three days I would relish the energy and live more intensely than I did all year. But with Diego, I felt only dread. As I introduced him to people, I felt as though I were hiding something, and I was oddly ashamed. I had walked in with 140 pounds of dynamite strapped to me that could hurt others besides me if it exploded. Nothing attracted me, no person, no body, no idea. I saw Jim only once from a great distance, a quick glimpse of his straight back and long legs. I didn't want to have sex with him. I only wished the conference would end. I dangled my ring before the funny man I had danced with last year, and he looked up at me, concerned.

I spoke to Curtis, a man I'd known in grad school, and in the most upbeat way, told him about our life.

"Oh, you don't want him to learn English," he said. "Then you won't be able to *control* him."

The accusation baffled me so, I barely felt the sting. Me, control Diego? I wanted him to find his own life! I wanted him to get away from me! If control were my aim, I might as well try to control Mount Etna.

Diego didn't erupt until the night before my talk. With sulfurous tears, he spewed horrors about how his friends had pushed drugs on him, especially cocaine. Diego's region had become a portal for cocaine into Europe, and when he'd worked at a disco, they had given him coke so that he could stay up all night. He knew of clubs that paid people in coke. I didn't understand why he was so upset now that he had escaped. I had never known anyone who took drugs. I tried to calm him and reassure him that he was safe.

Meanwhile, I was throwing up. We had eaten chicken the night before, and I must have gotten a bad bird. While Diego cried, my stomach churned and heaved. I lost count of the number of times I embraced the toilet. Three? Four? Diego seemed fine physically, and he barely noticed my disappearances. I presented my paper after a sleepless night and remembered nothing of it afterward, only that I didn't faint as I had feared.

Sunday morning, we went to church at the university where I used to teach. For two years I had sung with their choir, and at first, I had hoped we could marry there. I abandoned the idea when I learned what it cost, but not before Diego had told most of his town he was getting married in Boston. Since I couldn't get Diego out of bed, we missed the first two hymns, a tragedy since I no longer had a chance to sing. We heard the sermon—Diego demanded a simultaneous translation—and to my horror, it was about Spain. The minister joked about a rural Spaniard, and Diego asked me what sort of Spaniard it was.

"A shepherd," I whispered.

Diego stalked out of the church. From rebellion, or maybe from exhaustion, I refused to follow. I found him afterward in the courtyard, fulminating with rage.

"Where is this minister? I am going to tell him what kind of minister he is!"

Diego resented all insults to Spain and to his region in particular. American history consisted of lies written to justify thefts from Spain. We should all be speaking Spanish now, not English! We were only doing so because England, a nation of selfish hypocrites, had committed outrages against the Spanish Empire.

The cold in the courtyard chilled my blood, but still I managed to stall him. He wanted to go down to the basement, where my friends from choir had gathered, and bellow in the offending minister's face. I remember the faintness, the sickness in my stomach, the indifference of the redbrick buildings with clean

Laura Otis

white trim. By the time we went inside, the minister had escaped. The rotund organist said it was a shame that we hadn't been married in their church.

Diego drove us home in four hours flat, and his fury never subsided. Stiff and white, he cursed the ignorance of Protestant ministers who thought all Spaniards were shepherds. Now why did I defend that poor minister? It just turned Diego against me. I had been to Spain six times, and I had never met a shepherd.

Educational Services

Diego couldn't take free courses at my university until I had taught there at least a year. Since we couldn't afford tuition, he studied at Educational Services the first fall. In high school we had laughed at kids who went to Educational Services: kids who wanted to be hairdressers, mechanics, or nurse's aides. When I learned that Educational Services taught English for free, I quickly lost my snobbery.

At Educational Services, Diego met some unfamiliar speakers of Spanish. He had grown up making fun of "sudacas," Spain's name for South Americans who flocked to the imperial homeland seeking work. He had seen them as bums, con artists, and thieves.

"Who went to America?" his mother used to yell. "The worst! ¡Lo peor de cada casa!"

In New York, people couldn't distinguish Diego from a sudaca, and he suffered the worst crisis of his life. Until he spoke, his blond hair and blue eyes made people think he was an Anglo. But once he opened his mouth, he became a gardener, a dishwasher, or a busboy. "Spanish Food," said the supermarket aisle of beans, papaya juice, and guava paste. No one saw any difference between him and a salvadoreño.

At first, he reacted with rage and disgust. He was surrounded by ignorant bumpkins. Worse yet, the sudacas at Educational Services attacked his liberal views. They turned on him when he praised Fidel Castro's fight against imperialism.

"Fidel Castro is a killer!" cried one passionate woman.

Little by little, he began to like his Central American and Caribbean classmates. Some of their claims struck him as true: American women were selfish and didn't love their children. He adopted their opinion of African Americans, "the worst people in the world." He found it outrageous that his friends were seen as dishwashers, and he stopped calling them sudacas.

Diego made friends at Educational Services, but he never wanted me to meet them. Raúl, his favorite, lived on welfare. Raúl drank from a flask he carried around, and he adored his fierce older girlfriend. His son had gone bad—a victim of this filthy country and its lack of morality. The boy had bought drugs with the gold chain Raúl had given him for his birthday. How was it, Diego asked, that I worked so hard, but Raúl and his girlfriend lived in a nicer apartment? Raúl had a larger television than we did. Sometimes he gambled at the Indian reservation, so I said maybe he had won money gambling.

When the big snows came, Diego spent days with Raúl and left me alone to work. A man has to get out of the house, Raúl said. You can't stay cooped up with a woman all day. One time, Diego came home with blood streaming down the side of his head. He and Raúl had been shouting at each other, and Raúl's girlfriend had hit Diego with a statue, screaming that he had better not talk that way to Raúl. Until then I had wanted to meet them, but Diego had kept us apart. I suspected that I was the root of the problem. Raúl must have thought that Diego and I looked down on him.

"¡Primitivo! ¡Primitivo!" I exclaimed as I washed the blood from his face.

After that he didn't visit Raúl anymore. He decided that Raúl and his girlfriend were crazy. But Educational Services he liked. When he started at my university the next fall, I think he was sorry to leave.

Nervios

Diego said that I had "nervios." With the patronizing air of a nineteenth-century doctor, he explained that women were nervous and needed help to maintain control. To cure my condition, he would yell at me.

Diego did have a point. If I dropped a pan lid—I often dropped things—I screamed and stood gasping as it clattered to the floor. It would take minutes before I could breathe again and peel my hand from my thumping heart. I shrieked, went rigid and gasped when the window blinds fell in my face. About every tenth time that I pulled their white string, the cheap blinds clattered down, smashing my nose.

Diego came from a world where anger was allowed but depression was antisocial. In the morning, if I woke up crying with despair, he reproached me angrily:

"¡Qué mal humor tienes!" What a lousy mood you're in today!

I woke up crying because the nights were horrors. My first spring, I taught an honors course where the students wouldn't accept a grade lower than A. When I handed them back their first papers and asked them to revise, they responded with outrage and tried to bully me into giving them As outright. I feared them terribly, since bad evaluations could put me out on the street. But I couldn't give As to papers that needed so much work. I ended up crying and shaking with terror in the middle of the night.

"Take deep breaths! Take deep breaths!" roared Diego.

The way to deal with a hysterical woman was to beat her into shape. Back in Madrid, we'd had our worst argument when Diego claimed you had to slap a hysterical woman in the face.

"If you hit me, I'll leave you!" I cried. I was braver back then.

Then Diego had started to leave. He said he didn't know if we should be together, and I panicked. The world reeled as it did every time a man wanted to leave. Please stay, I pleaded. Diego wasn't the kind of guy who would hit me. I would do anything, anything, if he just wouldn't leave.

So I ended up with Diego yelling at me to take deep breaths in the middle of the night. My stomach clenched, and I dropped most things I grasped. I got more nervous all the time.

His Father's Ghost

On November 13, Diego asked to pray for his father, who had died four years ago. On the service road of the Holland Turnpike, I found a Catholic church, modern with dark glass and greenish bronze. Protestant by culture, atheist by creed, I waited in the car while he prayed. I stayed outside from respect, worrying that I would dirty the place.

Diego's father had left the world at the worst possible time. Raised in a poor family, he had made himself a lawyer through intelligence and brute aggression. Diego talked about him so much that he hovered over us as a living force. In every situation, Diego repeated his advice, telling me what his father would do.

His father's ideas appalled me, since he had used the law as a weapon to rule. Once on a highway, someone had passed his father on the right. His father tailgated the man at high speed and forced him off the road. "I'll teach you the law!" he bellowed until the man stood stupefied with fear.

Diego tried to pass on to me what his father had shown to him. If someone accuses you of something, counterattack; don't defend yourself; make him prove it. In our fights, even though Diego had revealed his strategy, it always worked against me. When he attacked me, I reeled with guilt and defended myself in confused stammers. Whether Diego was wrong seemed irrelevant to him. What mattered was to win.

At sixty, his father had developed a belly. He bragged to his friends how much that belly had cost, since he loved to eat and drink. With less than an hour's notice, he would call his wife and say, "We're going to dinner tonight." She would be expected to appear gleaming, a groomed conquest to display to his clients.

Only at the end, in tears, did Diego tell me about the hitting. His father had beaten Diego until he was well into his teens. Once, his father had punched his mother so hard, Diego thought he had killed her. I imagined what it would mean to live in that family while his father still walked the earth. His father would bellow orders, I would protest, and his fists would send me flying. I would go to the police and press charges, and the officers would wink at him and lose the file. In fierce whispers, his family would order me to keep quiet, to take my pummeling in silence. I rejoiced that Diego's father was dead.

Diego didn't. Besides his law practice, his father had run businesses where money slid between accounts and there was never enough cash. When his father died, the unsound system had collapsed. Diego was halfway through college, but his mother had pulled him out. He was ordered to come home and manage a real estate business. Everyone knew it would fail, but he had to leave school to serve his family.

Their way of thinking appalled me, with family prevailing over all else. Coming from a country where parents scrub floors to send their kids to college, I couldn't understand a woman with a live-in maid, a vacation house, and a sailboat who denied her son the right to learn. But in his family, the need to maintain appearances seemed to matter more than the children's minds. I wanted to marry Diego partly to save him from stagnation and waste.

Like his family, Diego craved continuity. His parents had determined that their sons would be lawyers; their daughters, wine merchants like their mother. For years they had badgered their children to learn the appropriate skills. They had produced one phlegmatic businessman, one real estate agent, one reluctant shopkeeper, and Diego. Of all of them, he came closest to being a lawyer. His father had brought him up as his apprentice, teaching him everything he knew.

Mimos

More than sex, Diego wanted mimos. He wanted to be fondled, cuddled, stroked, and caressed.

"¡Mimos," he cried longingly, "muchos mimos!" as I sat on the couch rubbing him, trapped under his deadweight.

I wasn't much better at mimos than at sex, never having had mimos myself. Diego said my parents stood like two stone statues. They didn't touch each other, and they didn't touch me.

"Scratch me!" he used to beg sometimes. "Scratch me all over!"

I thought toxins in his skin must be making him itch, since his liver couldn't remove the poisons fast enough. Scratching him didn't put me in the mood for mimos. All I saw was tumbling molecules.

I suspected Diego craved mimos because his mother had never touched him. With four children, a job, and a violent husband, she couldn't have had much time. Clearly, his wife should supply retroactive mimos. But who would give mimos to the wife?

When we reached home each night around seven, I changed into my chandals, Diego's word for my baggy gray sweatpants and drooping red sweatshirt. If some flesh was exposed, he would seize it, but I fought him off because I was starving. Diego felt insulted that I wore crisp suits for my students but chandals for him at home. I thought how much it would cost to clean an aqua suit—or buy a new one—if a spot of tomato sauce marred it.

Diego wanted dinner, but he didn't want me to cook it, only to give him mimos. Each night I persuaded him that if I didn't prepare food, dinner wasn't going to happen. He settled, then, for yelling about his day while pots boiled and I sliced dumb, helpless vegetables.

As we ate, we sat on the couch facing the TV. Diego wolfed down his food, then grabbed for my crotch. I pushed his hand away and told him to let me finish eating. Please, one biological function at a time. Everything I ate stuck in my throat and burned. How can you swallow when someone is pinching your groin? I had to fight his groping hands to wash the dishes—another task he thought would happen by itself. Then I made his coffee—every meal had to end with strong coffee—and baked three warm cookies from dough I kept in the refrigerator.

"Sí, oso, sí," I gasped as he ranted that our congressmen should be thrown in jail.

I felt relieved when he left me for the remote. He clutched it in his hands, switching channels at will.

"I have the power," he said in English.

After a few rounds, he settled for the loudest, most violent action movie, then continued to shout about congressmen. When I had cleaned the kitchen, he settled onto me with a triumphant sigh, the weight of his head crushing my legs. There was nothing left to do, and I couldn't escape.

"¡Mimos, muchos mimos!" he demanded.

Colonel Klink

L iving with Diego made me feel like Colonel Klink from *Hogan's Heroes*. As an American, I should have identified with Klink's creative prisoners, but I felt sorry for the colonel. Klink was responsible for men he couldn't control, and he had to maintain appearances. For anything they did—such as running a resistance outpost—he got the blame. Klink had to tell the general how his camp was faring, and if the truth came out, he'd be sent to the Eastern Front. Somehow, I managed to forget that Colonel Klink was a Nazi.

The general was Diego's mother, since he had passed from her camp into mine. I respected his mother more than I respected him. About sixty, frosty blonde, with his fierce, white face, she had built a respected wineshop when women could barely leave their homes. She had survived Franco, an abusive husband, three miscarriages, and four children. The third of them was Diego.

Once a week she telephoned me for an update. Often Diego called her, always when I was grading papers. He yelled excitedly into the phone, announcing things we'd just started considering as though they were planned and done. As I struggled to concentrate, my heart beat faster, waiting for his approaching tread.

"Go talk to my mother," he demanded. "My mother wants to talk to you."

It was no use saying I was in the middle of a thought. You couldn't keep the General waiting.

I did my best to sound optimistic, although I was briefing someone with a firmer grasp of reality than Diego would ever have. She was anxious to know how he was doing, and she heard disaster in my muffled responses. Her questions slashed like scimitars.

Once, toward the end, I burst out crying in midsentence, dropped the phone, and ran to the bed.

"You see how it is!" Diego shouted to her.

By then, my structure of half-truths had collapsed.

I continued reporting to the General even when our life had become Germany in 1945. After Diego and I had been separated for months, she demanded to know why I wasn't supporting him financially. I can still hear her sixty-year-old Spanish voice, taut with her son's searing rage. In Spain, she said, I would *have* to support him. I would be OBLIGADA.

I told her he had exploited and abused me for two years, and I wasn't obligada to do anything.

I never did get sent to the Eastern Front. That would have meant losing my job and moving with Diego to her apartment, where two of her children still lived. Diego had married me to escape it, but he always wanted to go home.

The Party at Ted's

Each Christmas, a professor named Ted invited the whole department to his house. Of all my colleagues, he was friendliest to Diego, so we were eager to go. Diego said we should buy Ted a bottle of wine, so we went to a liquor store to pick one out. Fear and sadness gripped me as Diego brightened. He acted just like I did in a bookstore, as though he had suddenly met his friends. His voice rose to an excited shout as he recognized one brand after another. Here was Gibley's! There was Stolichnaya! How much did they cost here? He pronounced the names joyously, with Spanish phonetics. At last he had found something familiar.

With the dark-green bottle he chose, we headed north. Driving was the worst part of Long Island. If you went to a party in Spain, you walked a few blocks, but here you drove an hour and a half. Reaching Westchester was no easy matter. It meant lining up for a bridge toll, finding the right exit off the Cross Bronx, and working our way onto a fast-flowing, narrow-laned parkway. Rain streamed down the windshield and blurred the lights. Struggling to read street signs, we threaded our way along congested roads lined with shopping strips.

Diego negotiated well until the end, and I admired him. Then a crisis arose: he had to go to the bathroom.

"¡ESTOY MEANDO!" he roared. I am peeing!

My heart beat wildly, and my breath came in gasps. Would he pee all over Nadia's front seat? I begged him to hold it and swore we would reach Ted's house soon.

"What should I do, walk in and say, 'Hi, where's the bathroom?'" he snapped.

On Long Island, this was standard behavior, but apparently in Spain it was not. Diego's rage ricocheted off Nadia's steel walls and pierced like deflected bullets. We had to park way up a long, dark hill, and Diego found a solution. Rather than asking for the bathroom, he peed on Ted's bushes so that he could make a dignified entrance.

No one noticed our wine, but as far as I could tell, Ted had thrown a good party. Diego didn't drink, and he didn't yell. He didn't leave in a furious rage, and he didn't say anything that could get me fired. At ten o'clock we escaped intact to face the hour-and-a-half drive home.

The afternoon wetness had hardened to ice. On the bridge, traffic slowed to an ant's pace, and we crawled past two crumpled, shattered cars. The accident must just have happened, since the stunned drivers sat strapped in their seats. No one had a cell phone back then, and we never thought of stopping. In Spain, Diego would have tried to help, but early on, in an hour-long fight on the selfishness of Anglos, I had convinced him not to. Under Spanish law, you can be charged with *not* stopping to help. On Long Island, as I had heard since childhood, you should *never* try to give first aid unless you're a doctor, or people will sue you for everything you have.

Diego didn't yell as we passed the smashed cars, surreal under the electric lights. *That could have been us,* we thought. We lived in a place where you could do nothing without driving, but if you drove, you risked your life.

Happy New Year

I knew Diego would feel homesick at Christmas, so I did my best to give it life. I cried when I showed him the little tree and red balls I had bought at Nice-Price. How I loved that Nice-Price Christmas section! I hadn't had a tree of my own since I left my parents' house to go to college.

It surprised Diego that I didn't get an extra paycheck at Christmas, since most people do in Spain. I told him that didn't happen here; in America we went into debt. Still, I tried to make Christmas come. At a discount store, I bought a gold-and-brown scarf for Rosario, teddy bears for his brother's children, and a porcelain candy dish for his mother. I packed the presents in an oblong box and sent it airmail for eighty dollars. Diego scolded me for not spending ten more to send it certified, since in Spain, theft was rampant. As the days passed and the box didn't arrive, his anger grew. I was cheap! I was naive and incompetent! I pictured thieves tossing his niece's bear in the air and grabbing it with rough, stained hands.

Since I knew no one else on Long Island, we spent Christmas with my parents. Diego saw this as natural; the trouble was how to pass the time once we were there.

Except for preventing my mother from killing herself, there wasn't much for a healthy person to do. Diego asked me to show him how to play piano, but his touch disgusted me. He hit the keys as though hammering nails, with no sense of the sound he was making. He had no ear and kept repeating the same mistakes, learning nothing from experience.

In the kitchen, my mother parked herself at the sink so that no one could cook without moving her. She must have seen it as her rightful place, and she thwarted our attempts to prepare food. It horrified Diego that we sat down to eat in the same clothes in which we had cooked. In Spain, looking good energizes parties, but dressing up hadn't occurred to us. After dinner, Diego went to bed and wouldn't get up until the next day. I felt awful for him. I had brought him to a place where it was better to be unconscious, but I didn't know where else to go.

For New Year's Eve, we returned to my parents' house, since my mother had done an uncharacteristic thing. She had invited friends over for the evening. After a lifetime of starving herself and despising people who ate, she had persuaded my father to buy a feast.

I explained to Diego that on New Year's Eve, I had always gone to a friend's party. We took turns hosting them, and it had been wonderful to laugh and dance with people I knew. In the ten years since I had graduated from college, and the two years since grad school, my friends had slowly dispersed. I knew people on campuses all over the country, but no one on Long Island giving a party that night.

Diego told me about New Year's in Spain. In his town, people ate rich dinners with their families. In the last twelve seconds before midnight, they had to swallow twelve grapes. If they could, it was good luck, and if they couldn't, no one cared. Afterward, people wandered into the streets, talked with their friends, and drank in the bars all night.

I liked the grape idea, and Diego laughed with me as we bought red seedless grapes at Feldman's. The woman my mother had invited had survived laryngeal cancer, which she had gotten from colleagues who smoked. She was trying to live a normal life, although her voice—a hideous, metal rasp—emerged from a sieve-like grating in her throat. She had found a curled wig and had drawn herself eyebrows, and I admired her spirit. My father sickened with disgust when Diego stepped out to smoke, certain that I would share her fate.

The cancer survivor and her husband talked gaily, but my mother made the dinner bizarre. She didn't understand the difference between her plate, someone else's plate, and a serving dish. She only ate food on one side of her plate, as though the other half weren't there. Again and again, her trembling fork advanced like a divining rod toward the rainbow cake. She wanted that brilliant, striped almond cake, and she ripped chunks directly from it. I offered to cut her a piece, but she laughed at me. After eleven, she started eating grapes.

"No! No!" cried Diego.

He quivered with outrage, but I could do nothing. How do you tell a woman she has to wait to eat her grapes when she doesn't know the difference between five minutes and five hours?

Diego and I drove off into the night, since neither of us could stand the horror. I wanted to save him from those sick, old people, so I headed to Adamsville with its lively bars. I was wearing the most beautiful dress I owned, moss-green velvet with a halter top and full skirt. I had bought that rich green party dress at the conference where I'd last seen Jim, as I wandered dazed in the cold after he left. To match the green velvet, I put on sparkly earrings and high-heeled shoes, so for once Diego approved of my looks. The black, frigid air was fifteen degrees, and I worried about frostbite as I crunched glassy ice.

The first bar had light and warmth and music. I didn't drink, but Diego ordered wine, and we danced a little. I tried to smile the way I always do in bars. What was there to do? We didn't know anyone, and we could talk only to each other. We left Spanish style, planning to move on, but the next bar was a crammed, black cave with a mob pushing into it. Its loud, unseen heart thumped violently, and I panicked.

"I'm not going in there," I said.

I have never understood why people go to bars. They are living, throbbing models of hell. They inflict horrors that offend every sense: smoke, filth-cloaking darkness, loud music, foul stenches, sticky floors, groping hands of the damned. Maybe they become more bearable if you've poisoned yourself until your senses don't protest. I refused to put poison into my body. Diego said I didn't like bars because I didn't like people, but really, I didn't like to see people poisoned.

When I wouldn't go in, Diego exploded. He had endured the cold, my crazy mother, and our complete lack of a social life. Now I wouldn't do this one little thing for him, go into this one lousy bar? No, I cried. Judging from the mob, it didn't look physically possible.

In the car, we circled in the cold, empty darkness, supposedly seeking another place. We passed one restaurant that looked inviting, but you had to pay $25.99 apiece and stay all night. The red-and-green restaurant glowed like a brilliant Christmas cake as we rushed on toward the mall. Sometimes we pulled over to fight, and Nadia shook with Diego's rage.

"¡Este puto país! I hate this fucking country!" he roared.

I cried and said that I was so sorry that I didn't know anyone. We never found another place to go. Diego's anger grew hard and cold as the ice, his unspoken accusations tightening. We got back to my parents' house around two and went straight to bed, but at three thirty I woke to find Diego shaking me. Terrified, my mother was rattling my door.

"I don't know where I am!" she cried.

She had managed to dress herself, but all her clothes were on backwards. Wearily, I took her to bed and explained that she was home and it was time to sleep.

She didn't believe me. She wanted to do something, but no one was around.

Diego slept well into the next day. Then we drove home to Jeff's house.

Ice

I tried to warn Diego what winter would be like. In the fall, when the mornings turned chill and wet, he said, "Oh, I know how it's going to be. In the winter, it'll go down to fifty degrees at night, right?" I laughed. His Central American friends at Educational Services laughed harder.

"Man, you don't know what's coming," they said.

That winter proved to be the coldest in fifty years. For most of January, all of Long Island lay under several inches of ice. Not snow but *ice*, so that one good push would send you sliding across your front lawn. Branches broke; cars skidded. The world glistened with terrible immobility. Nadia barely missed being smashed when a driver lost control, demolished two parked cars, and rammed a tree on our neighbor's front lawn. The crushed cars stood where we usually left Nadia, but miraculously, the accident happened while we were out at the store. At Jones Beach, people went skating—not on the water but on the *sand*. That place of droning radios and coconut lotion had turned into Antarctica.

Within a month, Diego gained ten pounds. He refused to go out and cowered indoors, begging for hamburgers and french fries. My father found him more repulsive than ever. When it snowed, I stalked out with the shovel and freed Nadia, who had turned into a gigantic marshmallow. Like a squirrel, I had to burrow through powder until I saw silver gleam and knew I was digging in the right spot.

Diego and I went out just once in January, to a party at a professor's house in Brooklyn. Diego roared all the way home about my colleagues' ignorance. Hearing that he was Spanish, one man had supposedly exclaimed, "Oh! A Caucasian!" But Diego's English was so uncertain, the man might have said, "Oh! What region?"

One day I drove out to watch my mother, who became obsessed with giving a silk scarf to Mrs. Jensen across the street. Like all the neighbors, Mrs. Jensen had helped her, but my mother didn't realize Mrs. Jensen might not want one of her grubby, faded silk scarves. Such was the force of my mother's will that she effortlessly imposed it on me, even though her wish was insane. I interrupted my desperate cleaning to find her box of scarves, drag out the ironing board, and flatten an aqua square that might pass for new. I have always loved ironing, the Darth Vader sigh that makes things smooth.

Suddenly I realized that I hadn't seen my mother in a while. I turned off the iron and found the front door gaping. Far out on the lawn, halfway down to the street, my shriveled mother was skidding over the snow. She didn't weigh enough to break through the icy crust. In one clawlike hand she clutched a peach silk scarf, and coatless, in the frigid air, she was moving determinedly toward Mrs. Jensen's house. In the frozen whiteness, she looked like a Caspar David Friedrich figure, a dark speck of life in the cold. Imagining myself accused of criminal neglect, I dragged her back in, twisting and mewing. As far as I know, Mrs. Jensen never got her silk scarf.

Work

Work is the most important thing in life. We are in this world to create, to put our bodies and minds to the best use. Whether your work is changing diapers, designing buildings, or teaching pottery, it defines you as a person. If you hate your work, you hate yourself, and if you think you're too good for work, you have lost touch with the world.

Work has always made me feel worthy of living. Since junior high school, I have worked every weekend, reading, writing, dusting, ironing, grading papers, planning the next week. When you work, you pay the debt you owe the world for your existence. As soon as I stop working, guilt closes its icy fingers around my throat.

Diego had a different attitude. He viewed work as a monster that chewed people up if they were too dumb to escape. The purpose of intelligence was to learn how to work as little as possible. Work dishonored you, made you lowly and ridiculous. Work was for losers.

I hoped that when he found a job in a country where work gets you places, he would change his mind. His outlook shocked me, but I ascribed it to a land that had 23 percent unemployment, where advancement depended on who you knew.

Diego's work permit came in February on a day of piercing, icy rain. As I fumbled through the mail, I cursed our landlord, Jeff. We had to share his cavernous mailbox on a wooden post at the foot of his driveway. Our daily shuffle through Jeff's mail enraged Diego, who had grown up with an elegant brass box by his apartment's entrance. To protest junk mail, Jeff left it in the box, and in wind, rain, and snow, we had to sort through weeks of his *Thrifty Weeklies* and credit card offers. Any of that pulp might conceal a thin, precious envelope from La Migra.

When my freezing fingers grasped the white letter, I almost dropped it down the sewer. Below the mailbox lay a metal mouth leading down under the street. When I was growing up, towheaded twin boys threw people's mail down the sewer until someone threatened to sue their parents. Those dark, magnetic holes exert a power of attraction that few thin envelopes can resist.

I imagined myself telling Diego the news: the work permit, for which we had waited six months, was floating in thick, black ooze. Diego would scream that I had done it on purpose and I was a stupid whore out to ruin his life. But I held on to the envelope, so that Diego could begin his quest for a job.

It's not hard to find work in the United States—unless you want a full-time job that pays enough to live on. Since my salary supported us, Diego's first work would be a learning experience. I hoped that he would meet people, improve his English, and break paths to new, more satisfying jobs. I wanted Diego to build a life that wasn't centered around me.

Almost immediately, he found work at Feldman's supermarket. The job delighted him. Each morning at six he put on a green apron, wheeled a basket through bright, empty aisles, and picked up peppers, apples, carrots, pineapples, lettuce, and tomatoes for salads. He cut them up and arranged them in silver bins. The deli, that was his duty. The store excited him, and he yelled to his friends in Spain about the enormity of the place.

Diego disliked his boss, a fat, older woman who ordered him around and turned sarcastic when he made mistakes. He understood little of what she or the customers said, but his blond hair got him a counter job. Despite the sounds that emerged from him, no one believed that he couldn't speak English.

At 5:00 a.m. I would flail away on my Nordic ski machine, then toast us bagels and make coffee. At ten to six I drove Diego to Feldman's, then rushed back home and took a shower. I drove Nadia to school, arriving just in time to teach my nine o'clock class. When Diego finished his salads at noon, he took the bus to my university, picked up Nadia, and drove her to Educational Services. When his classes ended, he met me at six, trembling with rage if I wasn't ready.

"What are you doing? The *other* professors are all gone!"

He had married a loser, a sucker, a fool who worked harder than other people did. My work habits embarrassed him. He suspected I was communicating with some lover, since sometimes I begged him to wait in the library until I was done.

We fumed and bickered on the Holland Turnpike as we played "Red Light, Green Light, 1-2-3." Twenty-six traffic lights between work and home told us when we had to stop and when we could go. Everything—Feldman's, Educational Services, my university—lay along that pipeline through which our lives ran. Behind it, shy wooden houses crouched on green lawns, hiding from the noisy world that fed and fueled them.

When Easter came, Diego wanted to know why he didn't have Holy Week off. He pointed out that my university closed for Rosh Hashanah and Yom Kippur, which had always struck me as natural. Why not Holy Thursday and Good Friday? The United States—or at least Feldman's market—was discriminating against Catholics! The Jews were running the government! Diego's suspicions were confirmed when his fat boss explained, "This is a Jewish supermarket." I asked him why he needed a whole week off for Easter. I mean, what would he do? Hunting for eggs takes only so long. But Diego raged about Jewish conspiracies. Nothing I said could change his mind.

In the end, his exploitation lasted only a month. One day he announced that he wouldn't go back. The fat woman was a bitch, and he was exhausted. The work had ceased to be a game and was no longer fun.

When she called to ask Diego where he was, he yelled, "I leave the job!"

Fine, she said.

That was the end of Diego's first work.

Popcorn

After months of shuttling up and down the Holland Turnpike, we realized we needed a second car. The public bus frightened Diego, who at first didn't understand what people wanted when they bellowed, "Back daw!" We couldn't have afforded another car, so my father tried to help us out. He had no more use for his white station wagon, and he offered to sell it. We transacted the deal formally, signing papers and driving to the DMV to change plates. Diego was thrilled. At last, he had his very own car!

But what a car! My parents bought big American cars that ran well for a few years and then collapsed. I called one of them the quantum mechanics car, because when you hit the gas for a tricky left turn, you never knew if it would go or stall; you could only quote odds. The white station wagon with maroon plastic seats had an engine so small, it accelerated more slowly than most trucks. All sorts of things ailed it, and it could die at any time. But Diego loved the white hulk: it was big, it was American, and it was his car.

"Espantaculos," he called it, scare-ass, but not because it scared the ass off you to ride in it. Graceless, boxy, defiled by rusty scrapes, it would scare off good-looking girls. The purpose of a car was to attract women with nice asses, and an ugly car was an espantaculos.

Sadly, Espantaculos took more time in maintenance than he saved us in turnpike relays. On Saturdays in Boston, I used to grade until two, then go out to explore bright, gleaming stores. Once we bought Espantaculos, Saturday afternoons went for the automotive shop. One time we waited two hours, only to be told by an Indian mechanic that we had a tune-up problem, not a battery problem, and we should leave. Diego raged, insulted, and threatened, but the Indian man stood firm. "This is not a battery problem."

Diego befriended the Latino mechanics, who advised him on which parts to buy. I knew nothing about cars and was pretty much useless, which enraged Diego even more.

When Espantaculos suffered injuries, he reported them with an odd glee. Somehow, one of the tiny rear windows shattered.

"It's like popcorn back there, all the little pieces flying around," he said cheerfully.

At the time Diego was delivering pizzas, and anyone who found glass in their pizza would sue. Diego made no move to gather the glass, so the next Saturday, I harvested popcorn while our clothes were churning in the laundromat. In the rear of that car, there must have been a thousand tiny crystal cubes. As the maroon carpet chewed at my knees, I plucked up diamonds one by one. Around me, the white oven stank of acrid dust. Gingerly, I shifted my legs to avoid being pierced.

Oh—there was another one. I pulled the sharp-edged cubes from the carpet, wondering what was going to break next.

Replacing the window killed two more Saturdays. I described what we needed at a glass shop, where we waited for two hours to learn they had ordered the wrong part. While we waited, we drove to a furniture store, where rain exploded with thundering violence. We swished back to the auto shop, but in the flooded parking lot, Espantaculos bottomed out and filled with smoke. I screamed with terror and leaped from the car as Diego swore at me and yelled.

The longer we drove Espantaculos, the more help the car seemed to need. Once he died in a dangerous area. I don't remember why we drove there together. For some reason, we needed two cars, and I was leading Diego out when I saw that Espantaculos wasn't behind me. I didn't know where Diego had gone, and the neighborhood was so frightening, I didn't dare stop. It didn't occur to me to turn back and rescue him—my inner badness, I guess, my lack of loyalty. Instead I drove home and was greeted by a message on the answering machine:

"You stupid bitch whore, you fucking whore bitch, what the fuck do you think you're doing, just leaving me and driving away?"

Diego came home about an hour later, having started the car with help from a gas station. He acted as though he hadn't left the message. He had expressed his rage, and I was supposed to forget it.

By the second spring with Diego, Espantaculos

was dying. He needed $600 worth of repairs. It was a gamble—pay the $600 and hope that he'd last, or dump him and stop throwing good money after bad. To Diego's dismay, I chose the latter course. I sold him to a junkyard for $40. Diego reacted like a boy whose mother had put his dog to sleep.

"¡Pero aún andaba!" he wailed. It was still working!

By that time, I had lost all ability to think except for a screaming drive for order. My father asked me about the tools. Had I removed the tools from the lower compartment? They were worth several hundred dollars. Tools? I had seen them once but didn't know what they were for. I remembered only an iron cross that looked as though a strong-armed priest could lead a crusade with it. By then I was doing everything wrong. My foolishness at losing the tools was just more evidence of my stupidity.

The Flat Tire

After Feldman's, Diego turned to Pizza King. They always wanted drivers. In a shiny, inviting brochure, they described the health insurance they offered workers after six months. I liked that they said not to feel bad if you screwed up—anyone could make a mistake. It sounded like a rewarding job if you stuck with it awhile.

I admired Diego, still struggling with English, for finding the addresses and taking people their food. He came home each night excited, shouting about shop politics. The local teenagers who did the deliveries grabbed the hot pizzas like aggressive animals. Whoever seized the most would earn the most tips, and that was where the money was. Without tips, you made less than five dollars an hour. On the road, if you couldn't find an address, you had to waste a precious quarter on a phone call. You incurred the wrath of the manager, who thought you were stupid. In the kitchen, salvadoreños who barely spoke English slapped the cheese, dough, and sauce together. One shaggy man slept in the store because even though he worked full-time, he couldn't afford lodgings. Probably he could have shared with someone, but he spent all his money on women.

One night, Diego had to close the shop, which meant that he had to mop the floor. He came home raging. He, Diego Ignacio Núñez Váldez, clean a floor! I mopped our small patch of black linoleum each week; cleaning the kitchen never struck me as an outrage. Floors had to be scrubbed. But in his house, the maid had done it. I remembered my mother's story about the summer she had worked at a bank. They had asked her to wash the floor, and she had, but then she had told her mother. Her daughter! Mop a floor! No daughter of hers was going to scrub floors! Her mother called the bank and said she was through. Then my mother had to stay home all summer, taunted by her mother and sister, who said she was fat, she was clumsy, she had no social skills, and no man would ever want her.

Before long the pressure of deliveries got to Diego. One night while I was grading, he rushed in in tears, still wearing his yellow shirt and crisp cap.

"I can't do this, oso! I can't do this anymore!"

He hurled himself on the bed, crying miserably. I tried my best to talk to him and find out what had happened. It was the usual: Long Island English, fighting for deliveries, and trying to find the unmarked houses. With my work window slammed shut, I fought to save his job and my precious future time. Four encased pizzas lay in his car, like yellow poker chips abducted from a high-stakes game. I told him to call the shop and say that he had a flat tire. Anyone would believe that.

"A—fla—tire?" he repeated the syllables. He had never heard these words before.

But he called, and they bought it, and amazingly, they kept him on. Even as I pitied him, my stomach curled. What about those four families who wanted their food?

Eventually Diego tired of Pizza King, although he worked there longer than any place else. They liked him and offered to give him more shifts, but even in summer with no classes to take, he refused to work more than twenty hours. I couldn't understand him. Didn't he see that we needed the money, and I needed the time? But Diego refused. The work had ceased to be fun, and in Spain, he had laughed at the guys who worked for Pizza Mobil.

Walking

When Diego started working, I started walking. His absence opened windows of time. Three hours, four hours, sometimes even five. I should have used those windows to work, and I often did, but those scraps of life were so precious, I had to *move*. In those hours, I could think and remember who I was. No one pounded, demanded, or called me a whore. I belonged to myself, and I could spend each moment as I chose.

In February, when the big snows came, I balanced on the filthy, crusted piles flanking the Holland Turnpike. I crept all the way to Nice-Price and bought a burnt-orange top and flowery leggings, dreaming of the days when I could wear them. I bought a strawberry cream heart that melted in my mouth and no one knew I had eaten.

When spring bloomed and my classes ended, I walked in the early mornings. Diego wanted to sleep until nine, but I awoke at six, and here again I found my own hours. I had to fight for them and wrench myself free. Diego clung to me like a drowning man and saw my abandonment of the bed as a betrayal.

What a joy to walk alone in the green light! On those beautiful mornings, the streets were tranquil. Locusts buzzed, and crickets sang on a high-pitched tone. Sprinklers hissed, and cars passed with soft swishes. Each day I tried to see something new. I admired the way people personalized their mass-produced houses. They placed dwarves, flamingos, and deer on their lawns; they changed shutters, installed birdbaths, and painted cardinals on their mailboxes. The Harrisdale people took pride in their homes, the first they had owned since moving from Brooklyn or Queens. The house I grew up in was twice the size of these, but my mother had viewed it with contempt. She and my father had grown up in 1920s mansions, and for them, the plastic tiles and Sheetrock walls were a step down. Unlike these Harrisdale people, they never improved our home, so that after thirty years it looked as bad as they thought it was. As I passed each house, I vowed always to care for my home, no matter how poor or miserable I was. I wondered what horrors passed behind each door, who was screaming and who trembled and cried.

When I walked, I felt strong. I didn't want to stop. My legs carried me at a singing pace. My thighs burned, my arms swung, and my bottom felt tight and hard. With joy I watched the summer come, and I marked the progress each day. First the crocuses bloomed; then the forsythia, tulips, and daffodils; then the lilacs and fruit trees. The azaleas flashed in brilliant pink bursts, and I wondered if I would ever own azaleas. Not until Diego found a well-paying job, not with rent consuming half my salary and disasters swallowing the other half.

Sometimes I even walked at night, when Diego

started to work late. I saw *Four Weddings and a Funeral* all by myself—what a thrill! I sat in the dark and just understood, without having to translate. Walking was free, and thinking cost me nothing. As I walked, I realized I was buried in a coffin, and I scratched and kicked at the walls.

Madame Bovary

That first spring, I gave my composition class a special theme: Adultery in Literature. So many great novels revel in rebellions that are centered on sex. My students could write about *Madame Bovary*, or even about *Fatal Attraction*. Most of them took the course for the 2:00–3:00 p.m. time slot. Three Chinese students clung together for support. At the end of the first class, one raised her hand.

"Please, Professor Heming, what is adultery?" she asked.

To me, adultery had always been a good joke, the triumph of biology over culture. But I learned that to Diego, it was no laughing matter. "Poner cuernas," he called it, to put horns on someone, a medieval thought in the twentieth century. To get horns was the worst thing that could happen to a man, a fate worse than cancer, heart failure, or death. Diego told me of cases where men had killed their faithless wives, then defended themselves by saying, "La maté porque era mía." I killed her because she was mine.

I don't remember when Diego decided that I was giving him horns. Probably as soon as I stopped wanting him. He began imagining lovers everywhere, so that anytime he couldn't see me, I must be fornicating. Spring semester I tutored a student from Antigua on Fridays from five until six. Diego smoldered with rage. What did this "tutoring" involve? How much was I getting paid for it? One night an Arabic professor walked me to my car, since women had been mugged and raped in the parking lot. Diego yelled that the professor was going to fuck me—if not this time, then some other time.

Diego didn't want me to talk to, look at, or be looked at by another man. If I didn't have to support us, he would have kept me under lock and key. Each morning we parted at nine in the parking lot, and he appeared in my office at six, white with rage. The other professors had all gone home! Why was I still talking to students?

When I made mistakes, he saw duplicity. I mixed up the days of our faculty meetings. If I told him we had one and then we didn't, he wanted to know whom I'd been seeing and where. Once when I couldn't face his anger, I intentionally skipped a meeting, and a senior colleague reproached me for missing a crucial vote. No matter what I did, I managed to make someone mad.

On my rare days of freedom, I paid for my glorious hours with days of accusations. Diego's rage seared like buckets of acid poured over me. If I went to the city to a museum and a movie, he accused me of fucking all day. He even believed I was with men while I was watching my demented mother. Once I spent a day at a shopping mall and bought a ten-dollar silk blouse and brown shoes. Who had I met there, who? It seemed

Laura Otis

unimaginable to him that I wanted to be alone. He never wanted to be by himself.

Diego's fear of horns reached beyond lived reality. We couldn't watch a film about a straying wife or discuss an adulterous book. This ruled out most popular entertainment, but the forbidden scenes still reached Diego's eyes. All hell broke loose the night we watched *The World According to Garp.* Normally I remembered which movies showed women with lovers, but I had forgotten Mrs. Garp and her student in the car. Diego especially feared I would do something with a student, since in high school he had wanted to humiliate his female teachers. He bragged how he had whistled when sexy teachers turned their backs; they liked it, no matter what they said. I told him it violated our authority and our dignity, but he never believed me.

When our microwave broke, we couldn't afford a new one, and at a little strip mall, I found a shop to repair it. For fifty bucks, half the price of a new one, a man could replace the microwave generator. I felt proud, since I hated throwing things out. Back in the car, Diego asked me what I was teaching.

"*Madame Bovary*," I said.

My answers had been shrinking, since the less I said, the less likely he was to get mad.

"What's it about?" he asked.

Before I could think, I answered, "It's about a woman who has affairs because her husband is so boring."

Nadia lit up as Diego generated searing waves.

"Do you take this as a model for your life?" he hissed, his white face inches from mine.

I told him I didn't want to have affairs, but he didn't buy it. I was mocking him in what I taught, in what I said, in what I did, with every person to whom I spoke. I was a faithless, fucking bitch, and it was just a matter of time before I gave him horns.

The Bartender Course

Once Diego could work, he wanted to try everything. Even before his permit came, he pushed me to respond to *Thrifty Weekly* ads.

First it was the phone books. Ten years ago, my sister had conned me and my boyfriend Jia into this scheme to earn quick cash. She convinced us to load the car with phone books and deliver them to people's doors. While Jia and I staggered with seven books apiece, she slouched along with one, smirking ironically. At the end of the day, we each earned twenty dollars, she having done almost no work.

With Diego, I volunteered to do the running while he drove and kept the list. I wanted exercise, since I feared I was gaining weight. But after hours of running with heavy books, my mind began to go. In Spanish, Diego yelled out strings of house numbers, of which I could retain only one or two. When I came back to ask, he got angry and called me stupid. I worried that my students would see me delivering books, since some of them lived in these neighborhoods. In the end, we gave up on the phone books—it was too little money for too much work.

Then came the paralegal course. For $3,000 of training, Diego could qualify to work in a law office. This idea made sense because in Spain, he had made it halfway through law school. My father offered to put up the money. But after almost enrolling, Diego balked. Deep down he must have sensed he didn't know enough English and that he would waste my father's money.

I tried to convince him that most ads were scams. Unknown patrons promised $300 a week for stuffing envelopes, and you ended up with a house full of paper, owing *them* money. Many of the firms charged fees for training, but finding a job afterward was your problem.

Diego spotted the bartender course in the *Thrifty Weekly*, but this deal sounded right. Here was something he knew—he loved the throbbing life of Spanish bars—and he desperately wanted to do it. The three-week training course cost $195. I paid for it with my credit card, and he quickly enrolled. How we loved that bartender course! Every night for three hours, Diego was gone from the house. I could work, breathe, unfold my mind, and he could meet new people. He came home each night shouting with excitement, showing me his cookbook and making me test him on recipes. He was going to be a barman! He called Spain and yelled to everyone he knew that he would be a barman like Tom Cruise in *Cocktail*. He was going to work in the coolest clubs, and he would get them all in and fix them free drinks.

I liked Diego's drink book. It reminded me of organic chemistry, except that instead of dimethylbutane, the end products had names like sex on the beach, grasshopper, or iced tea. Then I remembered what they were. These sweet, colorful liquids in pretty glasses poisoned people. They turned people into zombies and wrecked their lives. Cocktails were neurotoxins. That was why I never drank them and why I never went to bars.

Diego wanted to know why we didn't go to bars, and I tried to explain. Attached to strip malls like brown, rotten teeth, they were sticky, foul-smelling holes. In Spain, people live in bars, which have coffee, croissants, and octopus salad. People meet there at all hours of the day or night. In his town, he would wander from bar to bar and find a different group of friends in each one. On Long Island, you didn't go to bars to meet people, except for bookies, drug dealers, or hit men.

"They're full of Irish drunks!" I exclaimed at last, exasperated by Diego's questions.

Instantly, I felt ashamed. I was Irish myself, and I feared losing my job for this slur. Really, the bars served drunks of all kinds.

"The worst people in the world hang around in bars," my father used to say. "The scum of the earth."

Judging from the bars' smell and appearance, I had no reason to doubt him. His oldest sister, an alcoholic, had died blind from her addiction. When he was young, she would offer to "show him the town," whichever city she lived in at the time. Invariably that meant drifting from bar to bar, where to her embarrassment, he ordered colas. Their father would have to pay when sailors at her drunken parties smashed the furniture. As far as I was concerned, there was nothing cool about bars.

When I was a girl, my mother called me Carrie Nation because I said that drinking was evil. I sat in front of the liquor cabinet so that my parents couldn't mix their nightly cocktails. When I learned that Carrie Nation smashed saloons with an ax, I thought she was the greatest woman who had ever lived.

With my help, Diego passed his bartender test, confused that they didn't assign him work right away. What they did give him was a fighting chance: as long as he lived, he could call a certain number and hear the job listings each week. Often the number was busy, and he made me call it all the time. I didn't mind, since in another language, numbers and addresses are hard to catch.

There really were jobs, and each week we drove to the bars that needed help: a restaurant in Jonesport, a yacht club in Keene's Bay, a country club in Queensbury, and some kind of strip joint. The managers liked Diego's looks, but as soon as he spoke, it was no good. They took down his number, but he sensed their rejection and responded with snarls. The country club offered him work cleaning golf carts for five dollars an hour. Instead of taking it, he exploded with rage. No place that wanted him was good enough.

"Would you like me to work in a puticlub?" he demanded, his voice shaking with indignation. This

Laura Otis

meant a pussy club, a strip bar that offered additional services.

Hell yes, I thought, *if it gets you out of the house and pays ten dollars an hour.*

None of the places Diego interviewed looked like bars where Tom Cruise would work. Even if they had wanted Diego, he wouldn't have wanted to be seen there. After a while, I stopped calling the number, since the visits took hours and ended with outbursts of rage.

The Trip to Europe

E ach spring as soon as classes ended, I used to fly to Europe. I could only afford to stay two weeks, but I lived for those joyful days when I opened and stretched out my consciousness. In April, I started planning my trip. The funny thing was, I couldn't picture Diego in it. I had only a vague sensation that if he went, he would ruin everything, so I mapped out the trip as though he weren't there. I even reserved a ticket from Charter Travel and told him, as if he were a friend.

Diego's reaction was even stranger than my erasure of him. At first, he turned eerily formal. One night I asked if he wanted dessert, and he answered, "No suelo tomar postres." I am not wont to take desserts.

More and more often, he played a game: You have done something to offend me, but I won't tell you what it is. The fact that you don't *know* what it is means that you have committed not one crime against me, but two.

"Tell me," I begged him. "What have I done?"

But his thick, silent anger remained unexpressed and grew denser by the minute.

Diego started planning his own rival trip, loudly, irrationally, perversely. His intentions changed every day. One morning he would demand I book a ticket to Amsterdam; the next, a flight to Zürich.

After a week, he went off in a searing burst as we crawled through traffic on the Holland Turnpike. He seemed to plan his explosions in places where I would have to listen and couldn't escape. Often, he screamed as we rocketed at sixty miles an hour and the only way out was certain death.

"You fucking, whoring, selfish bitch! So you're planning to go off by yourself and leave me here all alone? I've been in this fucking country a whole fucking year, and I have nothing, *nothing*! My stuff is all in a pile in a fucking nightstand, and you're going to Europe by yourself. You fucking, whoring, selfish bitch!"

In some ways, Diego was right. He had left everyone and everything he knew to be with me, but what had I changed to be with him? I realized I could never go to Europe again, not the way I had before. There was no "me" to go to Europe, only an "us." I called Charter Travel and canceled the flight.

Hitting

Diego never hit me. Instead, I hit myself. I know it sounds strange, but I did it. Hitting is a habit, something you learn to do, a way of living you fall into.

I learned about hitting from Joe, my first boyfriend. Joe had attacks when his hate of the world loomed and crashed in a smashing white wave. Joe punched his face, first one side, then the other, like a boxer pounding a sandbag. If Joe beat himself in front of me, I threw myself on him to make him stop. Before I could calm him, his fists would strike me. Once he had to go to a dentist because he knocked a tooth loose, but he wouldn't say how he'd done it. Probably they thought that he'd been hit by someone else.

When I was a teenager, I hit myself for having bad thoughts. Back then, badness meant imagining sex with someone I knew. If I pictured my golden-haired social studies teacher on me, I slapped my arms until I smashed the image. If I weighed more than 108 pounds, I punched my thighs, hoping I'd remember the pain when I got hungry. Almost every man I have ever been with has complained that my thighs are too fat.

But that's not the same as attacking your face. You have to be angrier to do that. I first punched my face a year or so before Diego, when I tried to vote in Massachusetts. I mistook the ballot swallower for a card-punching machine and got scolded when I begged for another ballot.

"You have to *vote*," said an old woman accusingly.

I didn't know that in that district of Massachusetts, you had to write out the candidate's name. I went home and slammed my face until it was bright red and looked as though I had poison ivy. I thought I must be the dumbest person in the world, and I wanted to beat the stupidity out of me. Maybe next time, I would remember the pain and try harder to be smart.

Instead I got dumber. When I was with Diego, I seemed to grow dumber each day. I mixed up dates, forgot things, botched everything. Diego yelled about all of it. In my head, the hate became a straining thread, a strand of dental floss ready to snap. When it did, I would start to hit, but my hand never got farther than my own face.

I rarely hit myself when I was alone—I beat myself to communicate. I became my mother, broadcasting, *I'm hurting, and it's your fault.* The problem was, Diego never responded the way that he was supposed to.

I would start at the top, slapping my face with loud, stinging smacks. Sometimes I screamed like an animal. Gradually, my hands worked their way lower, punching my breasts and my ribs. I turned most brutal when I got to my thighs, the part of me I hate most. There I closed my fists and punched as hard as I could. As my hands moved lower, my voice dropped in pitch until the screams became a madwoman's gurgles. I ended by crying, sometimes for hours. When I recovered, I would go to Diego, whom I would find curled in fetal position clutching Bernardo, our teddy bear. He acted like a six-year-old whose parents were hitting each other, because in his house, they did.

The silliest things used to snap my thread. Sometimes it was burning the bagels. They didn't fit in the toaster, so I had to use the broiler, and they could go from brown to black in seconds. I couldn't see them in their hiding place where they were blasted by blue jets. If they turned while I was pouring boiling water, I was out of luck. When I yanked open the drawer and found them black and smoking, I scraped them with a grater, then smashed my face. "You're so stupid, you can't even toast a bagel!" my inner drill sergeant hollered. If I scraped them well enough, Diego didn't know about my failure and beating. Then I felt disappointed. I wanted him to know.

Sometimes the lack of money set me off. As our savings dissolved and our debt grew, I beat myself when the credit card bill came. When we bought a love seat and some Latino guys delivered it, I didn't have the right bills for the fee and had to give them forty dollars instead of thirty-five.

"They *said* to have exact change!" yelled Diego.

That day, I beat myself in front of him, screaming all the while.

Bad things began to happen to my body. After hitting attacks, I had murderous headaches. Red blotches marred my cheeks where my hands had made contact, and people told me that my face was red. More than anything, I feared I might hurt other people. Once I drove down Laurel Lane, smacking my face, right, left, right … I don't remember why I did it, but I could have run over a child.

I hit everything but Diego—even walls sometimes, but it never occurred to me to hit him. In one awful fight, he thrust his white face in mine, so that his eyes were inches away.

"Why don't you hit me?" he demanded.

How I longed to punch his face! But even then, I knew it was a trap. Once I hit him, he could take everything I had. It would give him a reason to hit me. So I lied and said I didn't want to hit him. It wouldn't have solved anything anyway.

On the back of my health insurance card was a psychological help number, and in April of the second year, I called it. I was crying so hard I couldn't make my voice work.

"I hi-it myself," I said.

Sailing

People always asked me what Diego did. At thirty, he had made it only halfway through law school, since he often failed his courses and had to repeat them. He had piloted his father's real estate business until it died. Apart from this, he had taught skiing and sailing.

Since these were his skills, I thought he could use them, and that first spring, I looked through the yellow pages. I found a sailing school in Treasure Bay, so we drove to the pebbly North Shore, and Diego convinced a man to take him out on a boat. The cheerful, heavyset sailing teacher had fluffy brown hair. I marveled at his courage, going out alone with an excited blond stranger. I had never had any desire to sail.

"Always watch out when someone offers to take you on a boat," my father used to warn. "It brings out the autocrat in people. A man may seem normal, but on his boat, he'll turn into Hitler. Once you're out there, he's got you."

I never doubted his word. Just the thought of perching for hours on a flimsy craft sent electrical arcs of fear through my knees. Why would anyone ever do this voluntarily?

But Diego loved boats. He yelled continually about

how his brother was letting the family sailboat rot. He bragged about millionaires who had paid him to sail their yachts to glowing ports and then bought him expensive drinks. He praised the beauty of the Mallorca marina, livelier than the miserable Long Island harbors.

Diego came back to land exhilarated, shouting with excitement. All the way home, he yelled about his future teaching sailing. After a few near disasters, he and the brown-haired man had gotten along well. The man had told him that he could, indeed, sail—the only problem would be communication. He had given Diego a book listing all the sailing terms in English. Diego just had to memorize them, and he could give him work. I rejoiced. Diego hammered. He would teach all kinds of people, buy a boat, start his own business, and we would sail around the Caribbean for months.

But Diego never learned any of the terms. The book slid around for weeks on the slippery pile of papers in his nightstand. He seemed to consider it an outrage that he should have to learn English to teach sailing. I asked him about it many times, but he only fumed. He never taught sailing, never returned to Treasure Bay, and never gave the brown-haired man back his book.

The Vermont Trip

Diego had taught skiing and sailing, and I never stopped hoping he would teach them here. When sailing failed, I thought we should try the ski resorts. We could drive up, spend a few days hiking, and he could collect applications. Maybe next ski season he could teach, and in January, I could work in a cabin while he was out on the slopes.

The trip started badly. Before heading out, I needed to mail an article to a journal. There is nothing worse than starting a vacation with work undone, so that you haven't earned your reward. All I had to do was print the article, but in those days, only one printer on campus could handle Microsoft Word. The fat woman using it was vibrating with panic. She had been scanning documents for two hours and had just lost everything she'd scanned. I had planned an early-morning, surgical strike: drive to campus, print, and race back home. When I returned at noon, Diego was shaking with rage. My selfishness had cost us half a vacation day. We headed north around two, so that we hit traffic in the Bronx and had to crawl most of the way. Near the Connecticut-Massachusetts border, we stopped at a Run-Rite Inn and fought for the rest of the night.

Sometimes memory offers form without content. All night Diego yelled and I cried, so that in the morning my face looked like a tomato and I could barely see. But I can't remember what we were fighting about. Usually our fights consisted of him bellowing what an awful person I was: selfish, ignorant, inconsiderate, lacking in social skills. Or he would attack the USA in general. He attacked, and I defended—so went most of our fights. In the morning, he reproached me for my swollen face and raccoon rings. How could I go out looking like that?

I dragged myself from bed, walked across the lot to a hamburger place, and bought two big breakfasts and hot coffees. I trembled at what that food would do to my thighs, but it made me feel much better.

On the way back to the interstate, we picked up a woman and baby who needed a ride. I feared it was a trick and we would be robbed and killed, but she was just a friendly lady whose car had broken down. She laughed when she saw Bernardo the Bear strapped into the back seat. On impulse, Diego had brought him along, the big, plushy brown bear he liked to hug. The woman said that he was our kid, and the thought filled me with fear. Children with Diego! No kids—at least for now—was one of the few things on which we agreed.

In Vermont, I reached the end of my strength. At a gray rural deli, where we stopped for food, I pressed the wrong button, and Nadia screamed. Car alarms on Long Island are a fact of life, but in the Green Mountains, they're an outrage. I had had no sleep, my period was coming, and I was shaking all over from the coffee. Nadia shrieked and wailed, and Diego hammered. Frantically I fingered the keys, seeking the button that would make the screaming stop. Meanwhile, a group of local teenage boys pointed at me and laughed. I understand now how people kill each other. In that moment, I was going to go over and kill them with my bare hands.

"Oooooh, better stop, she's getting angry!" they mocked.

Diego held me back, saying I was hysterical. He loved nothing better than when I lost control.

I began to recover when I saw those green hills. Raised in a flat place, I get excited by anything round. My ancestors fought with the Green Mountain Boys, and I loved this part of the country. Diego and I found a motel for twenty-eight dollars, the Green Orchard Inn. For dinner, we drove to Rutland and ate in an expensive restaurant—thirty-seven dollars for the two of us! Diego was happy, since the more I spent, the less angry he felt. An old woman eating heartily at the next table expressed her opinion of welfare: "Bread 'n' water, I say! If they won't work, just give 'em bread 'n' water!"

I had chosen Rutland for its proximity to Fleece Mountain, the biggest ski resort I knew. I had skied only a few times and hated it, but I had heard people rave about Fleece. The next day we walked up into greenness, with Diego shouting about the future. Excitedly, he pointed out the lifts and slopes, now shadowed by dense woods.

I had forgotten the flies. For hours, despite insect repellent, we waved our hands before our faces like windshield wipers. Desperate, I closed my eyes and sprayed the stinking stuff over my face and hair. Diego said he watched a whole shimmering cloud of flies rise up from me. Once we were liberated, we rushed along happily, talking under the trees.

At each ski resort, Diego took an application. The managers greeted him gladly and said they would need instructors when the snows came. The empty brown lodges stood waiting cheerfully, silent except for buzzing insects. At the end of the day, we bought a big bag of tacos and ate them while watching a soccer game.

The last morning, Diego got angry again. European holidays last three or four weeks; American vacations, three or four days. We stopped at a place called Vermont Country Breakfasts, where we were served by a tall woman with a big belly. As we ate, I sat choking with fear, the kind you feel when you're not who you claim. We looked like happy newlyweds on a Vermont vacation, but really, we were a nitroglycerin bomb. At any second Diego might go off, and I worried what would happen to the tall lady. I couldn't wait to get away from her and her Vermont Country Breakfasts.

When we reached I-91, rain pecked, then battered the windshield. Diego raced Nadia down the slick black road, cursing and yelling that he'd be late. We had planned the trip around his work schedule, and he had to deliver pizzas that night. At a rest stop in southern Connecticut, he ignited. With cars roaring by, he bellowed, "¿Dónde está el Báter?" Where is the Batter?

I didn't know what a Batter was. It wasn't a Spanish word I knew.

"¿DÓNDE ESTÁ EL BÁTER?"

I began to cry. I really didn't know.

"¡JODER! ¿DÓNDE ESTÁ EL BÁTER?"

When Diego thought of a synonym, I learned that he meant the bathroom. It was his way of saying WC. "Batter" was *water*, from *water closet*. No gringo, Latino, or Spaniard outside his town would ever have known what he meant. Why did he think I would know where the bathroom was at a rest stop on I-95?

As we crawled down the home stretch, past strip malls and diners, Diego's rage turned to sadness.

"Why is it that every place we go looks better than where we live?" he asked.

"This is where the jobs are," I said. I didn't like my answer.

Diego filled out some of the applications but never sent them to the ski resorts.

The Neighbor

E arly one morning while Diego was sleeping, a neighbor came to our door. Short and fat with a stubbly, gray-brown face, he looked like a toad. He was wearing shorts and a white T-shirt. A death-cone of ash smoldered at the end of his cigarette.

"Is that your car in front of my house?" he asked.

I said if it was a white station wagon, it was.

"Well, could you please move it?" he asked. "I pay six thousand dollars a year in taxes, and that's my parking space."

The tubby little man exuded aggression the way a hot stone radiates heat. I said I was sorry, and I moved the car, and that should have been the end of it. So why did I tell Diego about it at breakfast? Did I *want* him to fight for me because I was a coward?

Diego flew into a violent rage. He demanded to know the law. What *exactly* did the law say about where you could park your car? I didn't know, which made him madder. On the green curves of Laurel Lane, it seemed that you could park anywhere. The driveway belonged to Jeff, since we were renters, but the street offered endless space. Diego had come home from delivering pizzas at midnight and had parked in the first place he saw. That happened to be in front of our neighbor's house.

I could hardly breathe as Diego marched over to confront the man. I feared the consequences, but I felt a thrill of admiration. I had always been taught to give in to bullies if I couldn't avoid them, and I would never have dared to challenge him.

Shouts of rage tore the green, throbbing morning.

"FUCK—FUCKING—FUCK—FUCKING—"

Two voices battled with the same dull-edged blade.

"FUCK—FUCKING—FUCK—FUCK—"

I walked out of the house, hesitating with each step. Should I call the police? I felt an animal urge to defend Diego. The toad's mate was cheering him on, and I sensed that my place was at Diego's side, screaming abuse at her. But the whole business turned my stomach. How could I get involved in something like this? Fear and disgust kept me a spectator, and I never went past the edge of our lawn.

Diego came home, still erupting. He threatened lawsuits and said the man had kept repeating, "You fucking foreigner, why don't you go back to your own fucking country?" Diego regarded my disgust as betrayal, since I said I was ashamed to be associated with him. He was dragging me into filth that I could easily have avoided. Astonished and outraged, he couldn't see why I didn't support him.

The neighbor claimed he had spoken nicely to me. He had planted flowers along the curb and cared for the place he lived. Every day after that, when I passed

Laura Otis

his purple flowers, I longed to kick them to pieces. I imagined the yells, the police, the lawsuit. And so I never did. You can't go around trampling flowers to death. After all, it wasn't the flowers' fault.

Donde Viven los Ricos

B efore I married, Saturdays were beautiful. I got up at six, started grading at eight, and finished work by two. Then I could go out to see the world, take the Red Line into Boston, shop for cheap, sexy clothes that Jim might like, see a movie like *Basic Instinct* that made me hungry for him. When I came home, I could watch an old movie like *Mrs. Miniver*. Sunday morning, I got up early, walked to choir practice, sang the service, and graded papers all afternoon. Weekends had a holy rhythm, like the flow of time in a monastery.

Diego wouldn't let me get up. He clung to me and held me forcibly in bed, sometimes until nine, so that I couldn't finish grading until five. If we went to a movie, it was often sold out. He demanded to know why I graded papers all day, and I told him that if I didn't, I would be fired and we'd be out on the street. Five hundred bright, hungry people wanted my job and were circling New York's universities like starved seagulls. If I failed to prove myself, I wouldn't get tenure, and my life as a professor would end. Luckily Diego bought it, but that wasn't why I worked. To me, work defines, redeems, and purifies. It makes you who and what you are. If you don't work, you don't exist. I wasn't working for a better house or nicer clothes. I worked from fear of annihilation.

While I graded, Diego slumped miserably on the couch, watching TV shows he couldn't understand. I encouraged him to go out, take a walk, drive into the city, but he didn't want to go anywhere alone. He tried Manhattan a couple of times, but once he got lost in Jamaica. Another time he couldn't find a bathroom. In Spain, you just go into the nearest bar, but in downtown Manhattan, he could find no place to go.

"Estaba CAGANDO!" he yelled indignantly. I was shitting!

He had been forced to run into a restaurant, order food for eight dollars, then rush wildly to the bathroom. After that, he didn't drive to Manhattan anymore. Often, he came in and interrupted me, asking how much more I had to do. Once he crawled in on all fours and barked like a dog. He said that I treated him like a dog, and he wanted to know when it was time for lunch.

Lunch to me was an unwanted interruption, to him the bright point of the day. I would heat up a can of clam chowder and put a couple of frozen pockets in the microwave, or sometimes fry up two hamburgers. In the summer, he also wanted a siesta—more wasted time, more forced immobility. These could be nice, closing your eyes for a few minutes, doing nothing but listen to the birds. "Pajaritos," birdies, he called it, loving the gentle texture of that sound. When he took a siesta at his mother's place, all he heard was cars and shouts.

When I had finished grading, he was angry and despondent, so I spent much of the time begging for forgiveness. He ran for the car as a housebound dog runs for the leash, and we drove off to enjoy hours of freedom. Sometimes we went to Queens, like the time we followed Roosevelt Avenue to see where it went. Once we traced Flatbush Avenue into Brooklyn. Usually we drove up into the deep, green woodlands: Clam Cove, Treasure Bay, or Port Adams. Diego marveled at the mansions we saw—tranquil palaces in the woods with sleek horses grazing beside them.

As we drove, Diego hammered about how we would grow rich enough to live there. He would get his degree in international business, then work at home, fax, modem, fax, modem! We would move out of our Sheetrock house in Harrisdale, and I wouldn't have to grade papers all day. I didn't believe a word of it, but it was nice to hear him happy. He made wild, elaborate plans for the future as we rolled past chestnut horses with white blazes. Our kids would go to the finest schools; we would eat at the best restaurants; a maid would help me with the kids. When I tried to explain why this wasn't so easy, he exploded, so I stopped objecting and enjoyed the lovely horses and trees.

Trouble arose only when we stopped. In Clam Cove, he wanted to go to a dark, foul-smelling oyster bar, while I favored the clean, sunny diner next door. Diners had chicken soup and blueberry muffins. Oyster bars had slimy, ill-smelling fare and toxic alcohol. I won, but Diego's wrath and accusations made my muffin stick in my throat.

One fall day, we helped my parents rake their lawn, which lay stifled under an inch of yellow leaves. My mother insisted on raking, but she scattered the leaves with random strokes. She dragged them first one way, then another, cluttering an area I had just cleared.

"¡No controla nada!" exclaimed Diego. She isn't in control of anything.

My mother's sense of boundaries had been the first thing to go. She wrote addresses any place on envelopes, so that the postman refused to take them. She walked through the kitchen clutching a bunch of weeds with crumbs of dirt falling from their roots. In the living room, she left a rake full of leaves leaning against a wall. My father had been too depressed to move it, or maybe it had seemed all right to him too.

I can still see Diego up in a fir tree, throwing branches to me and shouting orders. Since I wanted to free the lawn, I grew frustrated with my mother, who then got angry at me. I was forcing her to do hard labor—she was nothing but a maid! Diego seethed with fury, since he wanted to get on the road.

"Vete al carajo," he snarled at me. Go to hell.

How were we supposed to drive together after this? But we did, dumbly, miserably, pushing as far east as we could go. Diego had heard about the Hamptons and was outraged to find that the ricos out there lived hidden behind tall hedges. We couldn't see their houses, let alone their horses. This would never happen in Spain! On that gray day we drove in widening loops, trying to glimpse something beautiful before the darkness came and we had to go home.

Strawberries
and Cream

One of our greatest pleasures in life was the drugstore at the mouth of our development. A cluster of shops marked the labyrinth's entrance: a Korean fruit market, a florist, and a marvelous ABC pharmacy. We used to walk down there just for fun. On Long Island, Diego said, you had to use the car even to take a piss. ABC was the only place we could reach on foot, and what a pleasure dome it was!

You could buy anything at ABC: pantyhose, light bulbs, milk, antifreeze, notebooks, plastic shovels, and pails. At a Spanish pharmacy, you could find medications and creams to melt your cellulite. You were served by pretty women in crisp white coats. But at ABC, Diego stood scandalized. He thought it was a riot that a drugstore sold cigarettes. I focused on the seasonal candy. You could watch the time pass as the wrappings changed color. First came Halloween, then Christmas, then Valentine's Day, then Easter, as tiny bars glinted orange and black, red and green, red and silver, purple and pink.

In June, strawberries fell to a dollar a box, so I bought us some for dessert. When Diego saw them, he wanted to know where the cream was. He often asked for things that weren't there but had been available at his mother's house. With hot chocolate, it was cookies.

"I like to have cookies with my hot chocolate."

With coffee, it was sugar. We were out.

"¿Sacarina?"

None at hand. He expected the house to be stocked, seeing no relation between the contents of the cabinets and what I schlepped home from Feldman's each week. He had the same attitude toward my body: he expected results without causes. He wanted me to eat what he ate, waste no time exercising, and weigh 105 pounds.

We made a special outing to buy Happy Whip. He loved the way fluffy cream foamed from the fluted white nozzle. I wouldn't touch the stuff, but he swore it improved the berries. I told him of people I knew who sprayed it on themselves and licked it off.

One night after some strawberries, he had driven to ABC for cigarettes, and as he stood on line, the worst had occurred. He burst in the door shouting that he was sorry, he had thought it was only a fart, but then *this* had happened. Our Happy Whip had harbored some bad bugs, and his jeans were full of diarrhea.

I helped Diego out of his jeans and scrubbed them in the bathroom sink. I must have offered to wash them, figuring it was my job. The jeans were too big and stiff for the little white sink, and I could barely roll them or work up lather. While Diego yelled about suing Happy Whip, I rubbed and rubbed until his voice grew dim and he floated far away.

Laura Otis

Costa Rica

L ate in July, I went to a conference. I traveled alone, and Diego was outraged. I had been invited to the yearly meeting of a group that studied North and South American literature. Each year they tried to meet somewhere in the middle, and this time they'd chosen San Ramón, Costa Rica.

At first, I thought that we both could go, and Diego called everyone he knew in Spain. He yelled that we were renting a vacation house in Costa Rica and they were all invited. Then I learned how much it cost to go to Costa Rica. A round-trip ticket was $700, but strangely, I never thought of not going. I had always spent my money on travel, and a conference was work.

"So this is what our savings are going for," snarled Diego.

I went alone, and the trip consumed half of our $2,000 savings.

From the moment I stepped off the plane, I felt as though I had entered paradise. A college town in a juicy rain forest, San Ramón had pink-and-purple houses with tin roofs. The town didn't have a single traffic light, and men at the market sold brilliant red fruits.

But that wasn't what made San Ramón so wonderful. For four whole days, no one told me how awful I was.

We stayed in the dorms, two to a room, and I landed with María, an Argentinian English teacher. The showers had only cold water and bugs as big as bats, but they didn't bother me. I felt rushingly, gloriously alive.

At five I woke up and went for a walk, to find the sun shining brilliantly and people working hard. By six, the place was bursting with life, and I raced past houses whose inviting red tiles gleamed through their open doors. I returned for a breakfast of papaya slices and great mounds of beans and rice. I had never tasted such delicious food. Every mouthful was an adventure as sweet, unknown flavors spread over my tongue.

In intriguing sessions, we presented our papers, explaining everything in Spanish and English. I did a simultaneous translation for a Canadian man—María and I were the best at it.

The first day, my libido flowed back in a rush. It had seeped away without my missing that delicious inner pull. My womb surged when I spotted two young guys from the conference, one dressed in black and the other in white, standing against brilliant green trees.

"You guys look like an album cover!" I cried, and they laughed with delight.

I wanted them, but I didn't want to have sex with them. It's hard to explain. For the first time in a year, I wanted to have sex in general.

I had seen buses shuddering down an unknown

road, and I wondered where it went. The second afternoon, pulsing with energy, I took off down the road. I walked off by myself with no water, no money, and no map. For hours I relished the strength of my legs. I passed herds of goats and bushes with red coffee beans. I crossed bridges over deep ravines and took pictures of soft green hills. At the end of the road lay a brown village, where I bought some juice in a shop. They didn't mind that I had no Costa Rican money and carefully exchanged my dollars. When I returned, I didn't want to eat, only drink glass after glass of papaya juice. I learned that I had walked twenty miles, all in about five hours.

On the free day, we piled into a school bus and drove all over the country. We visited an elegant church square, watched a smoking volcano, and swam in steaming hot springs. I was aroused by a Colombian girl who studied physics, and I swam as near her as I dared. She had shoulder-length black hair, lovely breasts, and Egyptian eyes. She laughed as she told us about how the Colombians had danced all night.

The only hard part was calling home. Each night I braced myself for Diego, whom I pictured bubbling with rage on the futon. His anger trickled through the phone like sulfuric acid, searing me as he asked whether I was having a good time.

I told everyone at the conference about Diego, since many formed halves of gringo-Latino couples. All of them sympathized and offered advice, but I shocked one of the album-cover guys. I told him I was preparing for the nightly phone call, which was like having to check with a parole officer when I hadn't committed a crime. He said that he was married too, but he never felt that way. He liked talking to his wife.

A Thousand Islands

After Costa Rica, I felt so guilty that I thought I should go somewhere with Diego. I remembered the Thousand Islands, where my parents had spent their honeymoon. My father's family had owned a cabin there, and I had grown up hearing stories of the Saint Lawrence River. Diego liked the sound of it, so we decided to go. But before we left, he took a language test at Spencer Community College.

The results said that before he could take classes, he needed to study English for two years. That sounded right to me. He had learned English in school, but only the grammar, and his spoken English was garbled and bizarre. Diego stormed out of the office in a violent rage while I tearfully apologized to the young secretary. She didn't seem nearly as disturbed as I was.

"He doesn't like his level," she said.

We drove north straight from her office, with Diego cursing "this fucking country." He never ran out of things he hated about the United States: the materialism, the vulgarity, the people who had money but didn't deserve it.

I took over the driving in Upstate New York as Diego's rage turned inward. I asked him questions, but he wouldn't answer, just stared sullenly into the darkness. In Watertown, we came to a tricky intersection. The route we were following turned on every other corner, and we had reached a four-way stop. I could see nothing because we were facing uphill, and the night was perfectly black. Trembling, I hesitated, scanning the void for oncoming lights.

"Anytime now! Are we going to sit here all fucking night?" snarled Diego.

I began to look for a motel, but he refused to communicate. In an eerie, absurd relay, I pulled into motels, ran to the offices, and asked about vacancies while he seethed alone in the car. I feared what would happen when he finally did speak, but he just went silently to bed.

The next morning, we crossed the bridge into Canada and reached the bright, cheerful town of Gananoque. Diego loved the busy little place. He shouted about the superiority of Canada over the United States.

In my head, I added up every penny we spent, determined not to increase our debt. The trouble was, Diego regarded every cent I didn't spend as something spitefully withheld from him. I laid out six dollars for go-kart rides, which I loved, since I adore anything fast. The boat ride (fifteen dollars apiece) was also well worth the money. The chugging ship carried us through cerulean water, past tiny green islands with gray fortresses.

That day Diego was almost happy, but the trouble began that night. We found a nice-looking resort with

Laura Otis

seventy-dollar rooms, but I said that was more than we could afford. We ate dinner there, in a warm restaurant with log walls, but Diego was so enraged, he stopped speaking. I tried my best to talk to him, and to chew and swallow. Diego answered tightly, if at all, and the food burned in my chest. By the time I found a strip-shaped, thirty-dollar motel, he had gone completely silent. He exploded in the night, and we fought for hours, well into the next morning.

I was a stingy, selfish, penny-pinching whore. I didn't love him and had never loved him, while he had sacrificed everything for me. I asked him what he had sacrificed, when he had been living with his mother at the age of thirty with no degree and no job in a land with 23 percent unemployment. I was a Protestant bitch whore, he screamed, and family and friends meant nothing to me.

I suggested we stay apart for the afternoon, and I took a long walk by myself. I thought of driving home and leaving him, but that seemed immoral, and it would make things worse. *What a crime*, I thought. The water was so blue, the air so warm, blessed with a sweetgrass scent. People turned the beautiful world into hell. How was I going to get rid of Diego?

The next day we drove into Kingston, a lively city with a handsome port.

"I thought Long Island would be like this," said Diego sadly.

We took a ferry to Wolfe Island, a place of green-and-yellow grass and peaceful farms. We talked of renting a house there, and of separating or divorcing. Then came the worst fight of all. We rocketed along at sixty miles an hour, our rage contained by the metal walls. We were almost out of gas, and I feared hitting someone, but Diego shot along, cursing and screaming.

"The problem is your FUCKING SELFISHNESS!" he yelled while I clung to the seat and cried. He took off his wedding ring and threw it in my face, so that it bounced off my forehead and hit the dashboard.

"I'm Catholic!" he screamed. "Do you know what this means to me?"

I tried vainly to withdraw to a place where there was no more yelling. I knew I had to get away from Diego, or I would die. It would be worth dying to escape him. On the way home he turned silent again, retreating to a tale of his own. In his story, he had been tricked into marrying a stingy, selfish whore.

Laura Otis

The New House

O nce we knew we'd be leaving Jeff's house, Diego
and I didn't look long for a new home. We couldn't
afford the Clam Cove apartments with varnished
floors, and the segmented boxes in Port Adams were
too small. One place seemed perfect, and we wanted it
right away: a two-bedroom apartment for $875 a month
in a neighborhood of densely packed wooden houses.

Our noisy agent said that before we signed the lease,
Fred, the owner, wanted to check us out. On a Saturday
morning, we dressed up and drove over for inspection.
It lasted only a few minutes. Probably, said Diego, Fred
wanted to make sure that we were white. I didn't think
so, since I liked the old man. In a barely intelligible
wheeze, he said that he had raised his family in this
house. For the inspection, he had brought along his
nephew from New Jersey, who had driven two hours
to meet us.

"Just pay your rent on time, and everything will be
fine," said the nephew.

I flushed at the threat. Why would a man drive from
New Jersey to put his uncle's tenants in their place?
He must have seen it as his family duty. I had met my
uncles once or twice, but I had never felt that I owed

them anything. On the way home, Diego and I made mafia jokes, since Fred had made his living in cement and wanted the rent in cash. But Fred was no mafioso. In his world, family came first, and a person's identity came from blood bonds. He lived in a world alien to me but familiar to Diego.

We rented the upper floor and attic of Fred's house, more space than I had commanded in my life. The pea-green wood-frame house stood close to its neighbors, its driveway running along Vinny's chain-link fence. The front hallway led straight to the stairs but offered some space to hang mittens and coats. Left of the hallway, what had been the living room was sealed off, since another couple lived in the downstairs apartment.

At the top of the stairs stood a small gray bathroom with a shower that drained into a tub. Through the tiny back window, I could see Fred's garden, where he worked each morning in summer. Next to the bathroom lay a miniature bedroom, which our double bed almost filled. The tenant before us had been a single mother, and her child had outlined the floorboards in red crayon. Fred bragged about what she had done for the apartment. In the living room, she had left her greatest impact. She had padded the floor with turquoise carpet and rigged white wire shelves in the closet. At the front of the house, over the main gable, hummed our little kitchen. We cooked on an old gas stove that I feared would blow up.

The best part of the place lay up the kitchen stairs, a spacious attic that we could use as a den or study.

Sloping rafters shaped the space overhead, and soft blue-gray carpet cushioned the floor. A window to the west looked out into an oak whose fine, dark branches against the sunset looked like the blood vessels at the back of an eye.

At first, I didn't know what to do with so much space. The bedroom should be next to the bathroom, and the living room next to the kitchen, but what would we do with the upstairs? Diego had lots of ideas. With a mind for style, he shouted about fashionable curtains and wall hangings, but every thought he had involved spending $500. We arranged the futon, desk, and stereo in the attic, so that it served as a study for me when I was home alone, and a den for him when I was away.

But that soon changed. Downstairs lived Tom and Carol, a brown-haired, blue-eyed carpenter and his lively wife. At five thirty each morning, right under our heads, they shouted to each other in the bathroom. Their laughter didn't bother me, since it was happy noise. They liked to kid around in the early hours. But Diego, still unused to hearing his neighbors, would wake up cursing with rage. He vowed to go down and threaten them, and I begged him to let me speak to them instead. We had just moved in. We couldn't declare war on our neighbors!

The ground floor emerged as a contested zone. Since the hallway smelled musty, I opened the window to air it out. Carol, who had grown up in the city, was horrified to find it ajar. She asked me to close it, since someone could climb in and break into their apartment.

The first time I did, but another time when I left it open, I found that someone had locked it from the inside. Diego exploded. They had invaded our space! They had violated our rights! He would show that guy! I cried and begged him not to attack, since I couldn't stand any more fights. To him, a neighbor meant someone to battle; to me, it meant someone to fear.

I liked Tom and Carol, although Diego couldn't stand them. Tom built houses, and Carol took the train to the city each day. I never learned what she did, but it must have been a job where you had to look gorgeous, since she was so lovely with her big hair and long wool coat outlined against the gray light.

Scarier than Tom and Carol were the people next door: Vinny, a Brooklyn garbageman, and his loud, friendly wife. Vinny owned a huge German shepherd that he had rescued from the street, and he talked about "n*****s" and the numbers racket. In the evenings, his booming voice filled the street, since he was friends with the whole neighborhood. For reasons I never learned, he detested Tom, and he bragged that he had torn the wipers off his truck three times. I lived in terror of what would happen when Vinny turned on us, but he and Diego got along well. Tom had offered Diego construction work, but he said no thanks, liking neither Tom nor the work.

We found a peaceful way to escape the morning noise, so that the war with Tom and Carol never happened. Although the only closets lay downstairs, we moved our bed to the attic and made the bedroom

Laura Otis

our study. The kitchen stairway became a pipeline of fear and rage, since we could never decide where the bedroom was.

In bed in the attic, I kept imagining the word *firetrap*, since the window was too small to jump out. In a house made of wood, paper, and paint, the flames would spread so fast that we would roast. I couldn't rest up there, and at some point, I must have persuaded Diego to move the bed back down. When I remember our nocturnal fights, I hear him stomping up the stairs and opening the futon overhead—*BANG! CRACK!*

Diego yelled that I treated him like a dog, and he wanted to have his own room.

The Toll

Three weeks after Diego landed in New York, my libido just died. I lost all desire for him or anyone else. When someone yells at you, you don't want him near you, let alone inside your body. I wanted only to survive, and sex seemed like a waste of energy.

For Diego, there was only one explanation: I didn't love him, and I wanted sex with someone else. I tried to explain I didn't want sex with *anyone*, but he didn't buy it. I still loved Jim; I loved the first nineteen. I had lovers everywhere: in my office, at my parents' house, at the mall.

That first fall, Diego bought a pair of tight red underwear.

"Let's see what sort of result this brings me," he laughed.

It brought him nothing, and he grew even angrier. At night he yelled, accused, and called me a bitch. His rights were being denied him. He had sacrificed his life—for this. After a while I gave in, since the fights took up more time than the sex.

Only a woman knows the horror of taking someone into her body whom she doesn't want to come even close. Sex became a stinging, searing ritual. Before Diego, sex hadn't humiliated me. Now it was a devastating surrender, a triumph of his will over mine.

More than anything, I hated his burrowing finger. Like an insistent worm, he pushed his way into my hindermost hole while I struggled and told him to stop. He claimed that I liked it, since I tightened around him, and he got angry when I yanked his finger out. He never believed that I didn't like it. Besides, he wanted his own hole. Nineteen other men had been in the middle one, so what was the point? He wanted his own hole, just for him.

When he mastered me, he demanded, "Say it!"

"I'm your whore," I whispered.

That was what he wanted to hear. Back in Spain, I had said it voluntarily, but the feeling that had inspired it had gone.

"Say it!"

"Soy tu puta."

The words rankled in my throat. I didn't say them—I threw them up.

Still, Diego liked it. When I said those words, he pushed harder and faster, and then it didn't last so long.

Sex became a toll I had to pay, like the seven dollars you fork out to cross the George Washington Bridge. It hurts, but there's nothing else you can do. On the other side of the bridge was sleep.

When I refused, Diego exploded with rage, sometimes in the middle of the night. He announced dramatically that he wanted his own room and stalked up to the attic I used as a study.

Bang-CRACK! went the futon at 1:00 a.m.

The house shook, and I feared the wrath of Tom and Carol. If Diego had stayed in the attic, I might have slept a few hours, but then came the cuckoo clock torture. Every fifteen minutes he stomped downstairs, thrust his angry white face in the door, and hurled buckets of sarcastic acid.

1:15 a.m.: "Gee, *honey*, that sure is a nice little nightstand you bought me, $19.99."

1:30 a.m.: "So, *wife*, you think you could spend some of your whore's time reading my job application? I know how precious your time is to you."

1:45 a.m.: "You sit on your ass all day, copy down two hundred quotations, and call it a book."

2:00 a.m.: "I'm leaving this fucking country. There's nothing here for me. You've made it clear how much I mean to you."

I cried and clutched Leo, a tawny stuffed lion. My heart beat wildly between the onslaughts. I wanted to run, but what would I do on the street at 2:00 a.m.? What do you do when the monster is inside? Diego was in my apartment, in my bedroom, and he claimed the right to be in my body.

Eurotrash

O nce I'd been teaching at my university for a year, Diego could take classes at half price. The students learning English as a second language there differed from those at Educational Services. They came from everywhere, but they were rich. Diego bonded with them, since they talked about what interested him: the coolest clubs, the coolest clothes, the coolest technology.

When Diego wasn't in class, he spent time with Germans who came from elite business families. They had been sent to New York to learn American culture, which would make them more employable and keep them away from their parents. They scoffed at their assignments, their middle-aged teachers, and their silly foreign university.

"America is all one big show," declared one.

As far as I could tell, they did no academic work, and they held no jobs.

"Eurotrash," muttered the long-suffering head of English as a second language.

Their tuition paid my salary, so there were limits to how outraged I could feel.

Diego told me stories about the Germans, who lived in a beach house with an $800 stereo. They schemed to evade the highway patrol, which expected them to drive fifty-five miles an hour. Used to the Autobahn, they found our parkways a joke and bought fuzz busters to beat the cops.

Secretly I liked these uncontrolled Germans, who saw everything through different eyes. One proofread my research proposal for a summer grant, and in their language, I heard my old, free life. I wondered what Diego told them about me, and I feared having them in my class.

At lunch they spent six or seven dollars apiece, but Diego only drank coffee.

"Aren't you going to eat anything?" they asked.

I should have been giving him money for food, but I didn't have any. Once our bills were paid, we lived on fifty to a hundred dollars in each half of the month. Neither one of us ate much during the day, and the Germans didn't realize some people can't afford to eat. A joint checking account hadn't occurred to me; if Diego had had access to my salary, we would have been evicted in weeks. He must have told them I was a stingy bitch and I was starving him to death.

Their refusal to study shocked even Diego, who asked what they would do when they had to write English.

"Oh, the secretary will do that," they laughed.

The last spring, I thought I smelled pot on his clothes, but I was never sure. Were the Germans giving him drugs? I wished he were back at Educational Services, but he enjoyed life more with these blue-eyed people who refused to work.

Paco and Pili Visit

S oon after we'd settled in our new home, Diego said Paco and Pili were coming. The semester had started, and I was teaching three classes, but Diego owed Paco, and that meant I owed him too. We had stayed in his place the night of Rosario's wedding, and he had roared up on a motorcycle when we escaped to the family vacation house. In Diego's world, houses belonged to everyone, and people didn't ask to visit; they just came.

From the moment Paco and Pili arrived, they never stopped shouting. They seemed to have swallowed megaphones, their voices were so loud. The first night, Diego ran off with Paco, leaving me to talk with Pili in the kitchen. Luckily, I liked her. For the past few years, she had been caring for her sick mother, who was dying of AIDS. Her mother had caught the disease from her father, a truck driver who stopped at puticlubs along the highway. Pili came from a region known for good food and wine, but she worried about her weight. Shaking the kitchen with her voice, she unpacked delicacies they had brought, cans of soft red peppers stuffed with spicy brown paste.

Unsure what to feed them, I mashed pizza dough

all the way to the edges of a cookie sheet. The men returned from a bar, vibrating with energy.

"Wonderful!" cried Paco. "The simplest things! A little cheese, some tomato—what else does one need?"

After a few days, we fell into a pattern I could live with. Diego and I got up, used the bathroom, and drove to school. Once we'd left, Paco and Pili emerged and took the train to the city. We hardly saw them at all.

When we encountered them, they spewed observations and questions. It was so hard to find fresh produce, to buy a salad not smothered in dressing! Didn't I like fruit? Why was there no fruit in the house? In their town, maids bought fresh fruit at the market each day. Why were there so many Jews in New York? From the bus windows they had seen them with those long curls dangling beside their faces. Pili mimicked a woman seized by spirits at a Harlem church service, which they'd attended on another tour. Why didn't we go rollerblading? Rollerblades were so cheap here! I tried to explain that I worked all weekend and that more than half my salary went for rent. Because they lived with their mothers, they could spend their money as they chose.

The second week, our two worlds came together in a trip to Adamsville. A professor from anthropology had invited us to dinner at a place with live jazz. For an hour and a half, until just before we left, Paco and Pili occupied the bathroom. Diego and I were forced to go dirty, and he yelled and cursed at me to hurry.

What would my friends think? How would I get tenure? JODER, fuck it all, hurry!

For an hour and a quarter, I drove us through blackness and pounding rain. I crushed Nadia's accelerator and nudged her between lanes even though I could see nothing but spray. Her walls vibrated with shouts as we swished through the wet night. We arrived half an hour late, so that the others had begun to worry. From the din of the car, we moved to the musical battering of a full restaurant.

When the anthropologist spoke to me, I smiled and strained to hear. I rarely could, and he soon gave up. Pummeled by the Spaniards, my brain could barely register another person's words. Why was she smiling, that fat jazz singer? Didn't the noise hurt her too? What was there going on to be so happy about?

After three hours, I knew I was going to cry, so I fled to the bathroom. I have never been able to control the hot, swelling sensation, the sense of overflow from inside. I chose a booth, sat down, and let the tears flow. But outside the door stood a line of itching women, and I realized with horror that I couldn't cry. I could flee into the night, reclaim Nadia, drive to my parents' house, run to the woods until the yelling monsters went back to Spain. But I imagined the consequences: Diego's rage, Paco and Pili's bewilderment, the scalding reports back in Diego's town …

No. There was nowhere to hide. There was no place I could go to get away.

When I came back out, they were calculating the check.

"El chupito!" cried Pili, demanding her after-dinner drink.

Paco was appalled at the anthropologist's choice to reckon expenses separately. He explained to me how to calculate the 15 percent tip.

"It's easy!" he bellowed.

My tears flowed.

When Paco and Pili left, they gave us a gift from a museum, a ceramic cat with a bobbing head. We both liked it and nudged its gray chin to make it nod. Then, a week later, I smashed it with the vacuum cleaner. Somehow, the plastic hose grazed the cat's face, sending the head flying across the room. When I picked it up, a star-shaped bash had blossomed between the eyes. Diego bellowed with rage, sensing betrayal. He never believed I broke anything by accident. I bought some superglue and, in a fit of thoughtless energy, stuck the shards clumsily together. The cat survived, its scarred head bobbing on the living room bookcase all that fall, winter, and spring. The night Diego left, I put the cat out with the trash, but still I couldn't smash it. Someone might want it, I thought, so I left the clay cat nodding next to the newspapers in the rain.

Tuesdays

T he second year, I spent Tuesdays with my mother. For my father, it was the least I could do. I taught Mondays, Wednesdays, and Fridays, and my father paid companions to watch my mother while he worked, so it made sense for me to come on Tuesdays. Diego would never have tolerated losing me on the weekend.

On Tuesdays I got up at six, flailed away on my Nordic ski machine, took a shower, made breakfast, and roused Diego at eight. He began yelling halfway through his coffee and shouted as he drove us to school. The Democrats who had voted with the Republicans should be thrown out of office! In Spain, such treason wouldn't be tolerated! I pleaded with him to hurry, since my father couldn't leave for work until I arrived. If I tore wildly down the parkway, I could reach my parents' house by 9:40. This got my father to work at 10:20, if he had his car warmed up in the driveway.

From the moment the sound of his motor faded, I took charge of a demanding seventy-six-pound woman. Each day she repeated a refrain at thirty-second intervals, like a mad clock whose chimes varied with her mood.

Usually she asked, "When is Dad coming home?"

Her concept of time had deliquesced, so that three minutes or three days meant the same vague deferral. What mattered was that Dad was not here *now*, and she wanted him.

"When is Dad coming home?"

All day long, I counted the hours and minutes, but the numbers rolled off her mind.

"When is Dad coming home?"

As soon as I could, I began to clean. Since I'd come home to chaos a year ago, I had made heartening progress. Each week I removed the growth of mail, crusted dishes, abandoned papers, and wadded clothes that had accumulated in seven days. Then I attacked a festering sump of disorder: the linen closet; the medicine cabinet; the maps, postcards, and brochures that filled dresser drawers. I dusted, vacuumed, and washed Diego's and my laundry, which I brought along in a straw basket. I pictured my sister smirking at this, but when you rent, you don't own a washing machine. My parents' washer saved me hours at the laundromat, and its distant churning comforted me.

If I had only cleaned, Tuesdays might have been therapeutic, but my mother sabotaged my work. She didn't want me to notice anything but her, but there was more to it than that. I was straightening *her* mess. She had always hated my cleaning, and with fiendish cunning, she thwarted my progress. She lost things: her book, her pen, her key, so that I had to stop work and search. She clutched a greasy key in her rigid white fingers, because she remembered that something awful happens if you lose your key. She wouldn't put the key down even to eat. She cradled books in her arms and carried them from room to room, although she could no longer read. Sometimes she lost herself and cried for help, wanting to know where she was.

On bad days she chanted a different refrain: "I want to slit my throat."

I sorted dusty postcards that smelled of bad breath and rotting skin while she recited endlessly, "I want to slit my throat."

"Come on, Mom, that's not a good thing to do," I said. "You don't want to do that."

"I want to slit my throat."

It certainly sounded as if she did. Sometimes I wished she would.

One week I scrubbed the shower in my parents' master bathroom. In this moldy blue maelstrom, bad feelings had always swirled. My parents had had their one and only fight when my father had caulked the dark seams without cleaning them first, so that black mildew was preserved under clear goo. A few days ago, my mother had shat in the shower, then laughed as my father wiped it up. My sister swore my mother had developed her dementia just to torment us. My mother had always wanted revenge, since we kept her from living the intellectual life that she craved.

With a brush and a bottle of bleachy foam, I wedged myself into the shower. Systematically, I scoured the walls and floor. But my mother, who followed me like a puppy, forced herself in behind me and scrubbed next to me so that I couldn't maneuver.

"Why don't you wait outside, Mom? I can do this," I said a hundred times.

"Can we stop now?" she panted. "When is Dad coming home?"

She had lost her cloth and was rubbing the wall with her hand, always the same encrusted tile.

"It hurts," she whimpered.

When I refused to quit scrubbing, she threw a tantrum and cried.

"I want my husband!" she yelled, kicking a fan that my father had left in the bedroom all winter.

I never finished scrubbing the shower.

At six I stopped cleaning, dissatisfied with my progress, and cooked dinner for three. The kitchen made me sadder than any other part of the house, with its corn stick pans, cookie cutters, pastry blenders, and egg poachers. It could have served a family of twelve, and the waste of that house made my stomach ache. I longed to bring the place to life again, and with each dinner I cooked, I tried to recover a lost item.

Once I found some old tapioca and made pudding. It was an enormous success.

"It's creamy," murmured my mother. For five full minutes, she stopped saying she wanted to slit her throat.

Usually the food stuck and burned in my chest as she vowed to kill herself, and my father and I took turns telling her not to. Sometimes she attacked him while he was eating and tried to claw him with her fingers. Her swipes at him reminded me of my sister, who at thirteen had grown her nails long and tried to claw us too.

At seven thirty I folded wash as quickly as I could. My father helped me, since both of us worried about Diego's wrath if I came home late. By eight I had to be on my way, the clothes neatly folded in the basket. But often, I stopped at Feldman's to do the weekly shopping. At supermarkets I sometimes dared to think. As I bought the food Diego wanted (cola, chips, coffee), I thought how it would feel to fill a cart with only things that I liked. Suppose Diego just weren't there? Never again would I spend money on chips or see bottles of soda in my refrigerator.

At eleven I staggered upstairs with the groceries and laundry. Diego lay slumped on the couch, the TV blaring out his anger. Simultaneously, he wanted me to fondle him, talk to him, and cook for him. I just wanted to put away the food and clothes. When I didn't comply, an explosion flashed. I was a fucking bitch who didn't care about him.

Usually Diego had some special project that had to be dealt with right then. One night he had decided to become a Spanish teacher, because teachers had three months of vacation. What courses would he need to become a teacher? When I said I didn't know, he screamed. Another time he wanted to know what Windows was, and I couldn't tell him, because I used a Mac. He took my ignorance as a refusal to explain, and he blew up in my face.

One night at eleven, I refused to cook him a steak. I had to be up in seven hours to teach three classes. Why hadn't he cooked it himself?

The next day I found a note in my office mailbox:

"Gee, *honey*, you could not cook a stake for your husband, I gess that would be too moch work for you, you are so bisy with important things."

I tore it up and went back to work, glad there was a whole week until next Tuesday.

Seeing Leaves

For my birthday in our second year together, I wanted to see bright New England leaves. Columbus Day weekend promised to be warm, the perfect weather to drive north. We planned to get up early Saturday morning and then just improvise.

At 3:30 a.m., our downstairs neighbors' TV erupted. Diego bolted up yelling, wild with rage. He demanded that I call the landlord to come and turn it off. If he didn't, he would break in and silence it personally. The house's wooden beams were quivering from the roar.

I cried and gasped and pleaded and begged. I couldn't call a seventy-five-year-old man at three thirty in the morning. I knew right away what must have happened. Tom and Carol had left for the weekend and had set the TV timer so that people would think they were home and not break in. They had just gotten the time—and the volume—terribly wrong. We would have to stand it until the monster turned itself off. Diego bellowed and threatened. Then, an hour later, the noise stopped.

I made breakfast, and weary and shell-shocked, we drove up the Taconic Parkway. Dazzling red, yellow, and orange flanked the road, and we began to feel alive again. We stopped at a park called Three Corners where New York meets Connecticut and Massachusetts. Laughing and talking, we took a long walk with those brilliant leaves shining above us.

Around three we started to look for a motel. The roads hummed with cars, and busloads of tourists overran the towns on Route 7. Run-Rite Inn and Travelodge had No Vacancy signs. By seven I began to worry. The darkness deepened, and we sped through northern Connecticut's black woods. No Vacancy. No Vacancy. No Vacancy.

Diego turned vicious, ugly, and mean. As I drove, my heart pounded, and tears brimmed. He yelled that America couldn't handle mass tourism, that we had no idea how to house and feed people. In irrational despair, we drove to Boston, where we found no shelter downtown or in the suburbs. Around and around we drove, off the highway, then back onto the highway.

"At driving around in circles we're very good," snarled Diego.

In the screaming tension of electric lights, a desperate woman told me there were no rooms anywhere in the Northeast. Virtually everyone had come to see the leaves, and every motel was full.

We could do nothing but drive back home, four hours down I-95. With Diego in a rage, I feared for my life. A huge black pickup roared by at ninety miles an hour.

"That one is definitely drunk," said Diego as the black torpedo shot past.

We got home at three thirty in the morning, having

driven a thousand miles and been up for twenty-four hours.

Diego loved it when I failed, and he told everyone about it.

My sister patronized, "You *always* have to make a reservation."

Diego's English teacher said, "There are nice leaves around here too."

Rather than gaining respect and maturity by getting married, I had sunk a notch. I had become a newlywed, someone who can do nothing right and urgently needs other people's advice.

New Orleans

When it came time for my literature conference the second fall, ages seemed to have passed since the Boston meeting. The world had kept turning, but I had slipped off and was flailing in space, watching it recede. I had fallen into another dimension, and passing that yearly marker reminded me that I was floating in blackness.

I went to the conference, but this time it caused more trouble. It was in New Orleans, a thousand miles and $300 away. We couldn't both afford to go, so I traveled alone, and Diego raged at my selfishness.

To save money, I didn't stay at the conference hotel. I found a ramshackle place in *Backpack USA* for thirty-five dollars a night. They offered breakfast but had no phones in the rooms, and Diego knew what that meant: I was fucking all the men at the conference.

The real source of his rage was that Jim would be there. He would have his wife and son with him, but I would be unguarded. I hadn't spoken to Diego about Jim since Spain, but Diego believed I still wanted him. Him, and any other man at the conference who would have me.

On a gray morning in November, Diego drove me to LaGuardia, dodging potholes on the expressway. I navigated, but the map contradicted the signs. To reach the airport, the road signs said to go straight; the map, to turn, and I had to make a split-second decision.

"Tell me what to do!" yelled Diego.

I went with the map, and immediately we were lost in Queens. The flight was leaving in an hour, and there was no sign of an airport. Diego bellowed accusations. With tears streaming down my face, I reached for the New York atlas and with my last remaining reason got us to LaGuardia. The fear of missing Jim motivated me most strongly. I didn't think I could go on living without him.

Diego seethed as I slammed the door and walked sadly to the terminal. I wondered how red my eyes were. In my maroon raincoat, I must have looked red all over. I had bought that coat four conferences ago when I had seen Jim's wife. Then I realized that Diego was gone. For four whole days I could breathe and move, but the fear of him had me paralyzed. What would he be like when I came back? I tried not to think of it. As the plane roared upward, all I thought about was Jim.

My red hotel stood bravely in an intimidating neighborhood. At the conference hotel, the clerk told me point-blank not to wander off of St. Charles Avenue. On the side streets I could get mugged or worse. What a crazy city! St. Charles, the main pipeline with a streetcar, connected the green neighborhoods with the French Quarter. On the cross streets, mansions had devolved into tenements. My hotel lay on one of these shaded streets.

Frightening as it was, I couldn't hate the city. In

November, the air smelled of flowers and wet leaves. As I walked down St. Charles, teenage boys hooted at my coat: "Oooooh, I'm cold!"

I stripped off the maroon raincoat, realizing that I was hot. When I sat at a café, I heard only the clink of dishes and the sigh of wind in nearby trees. No voice yelled at me that I was awful, and I read peacefully as I sipped my tea.

About the conference I remember nothing, only the hallways between sessions. Where was Jim? When would I see him? Would I find him around the next corner?

When I did meet Jim at the book exhibit, we generated an electric field that repelled everyone nearby. People felt the energy between us and left—it has always been that way. Jim looked as beautiful as ever, broad shoulders, straight back, long legs. On autopilot, I chattered to him about my book, my teaching, and my marriage.

"Sounds as if your life is starting to gel," he said, and I looked up into his eyes.

When I talk to Jim, I lean my head all the way back so that I can see his radiant face. The change in posture opens my mind, as if I were talking to a giant Buddha. I stopped in midsentence. I couldn't lie anymore, although I couldn't talk either. My eyes filled with tears. Struggling to find words, I started to tell him the truth. With everyone watching, he took me by the hand and led me to some nearby chairs.

"I—I—don't want to bother you—" I stammered, tears running into the corners of my mouth.

"You're not bothering me," he said quietly.

The rare beauty of Jim is that emotions don't disturb him. Tears don't make him angry or embarrassed. He just accepts the grief and wants to hear what you have to say.

For the first time since I had married Diego, I said what I felt. Until then I hadn't dared. I had had no chance. Like a person in a cult, I was never alone. Anytime a friend called, which was less and less, Diego hovered beside me, and when the friend asked, "How's everything with Diego?" I said, "Fine." In the hours I had to myself, I tried desperately to work. Gradually I lost contact with anyone but Diego. He liked this, since he didn't want me to know anyone but him. To my father I said nothing, since his life was horror, and I didn't want to make him more miserable. There was something else too—you're not supposed to hate marriage. If you do, you're a bad, selfish person. So I lied out of guilt and fear, the main reasons I've done most things in life. But with Jim I couldn't lie.

When I had told him enough, he pulled me to him and wrapped his warm arms around me. He held me against him, and his solid chest rose and fell under my wet cheek. He couldn't tell me what to do, but he could show me that he cared. I didn't get another chance to talk to him alone.

I ate lunch with a funny man from Michigan who remembered me from Costa Rica.

"Never seen anything like it! She just walked off into the jungle!" he cried.

I smiled faintly, remembering my strength the summer before. As I walked around New Orleans, I felt as though I'd been weakened by a gripping illness. I bought a tape of jaunty Cajun music I heard playing in a souvenir shop. I didn't go to the conference dance I loved, because I feared walking home at night. I had been mugged before, and I knew the feel of a man's fist slamming my face. At night I bought food at the pharmacy next door and spread it out on my bed. I stroked a pecan caramel turtle, read how many calories and grams of fat were in it, and thought how terrible I was.

Each night I called on the lobby pay phone, since I was only out on parole. Diego cursed and accused and sounded mad with rage. I had done this on purpose, picked a place with no phone. Who was in my room now? No one but the turtle.

The next evening, I had dinner with Elaine, an older woman who liked my work. As we waited for her husband to pick us up, Jim suddenly materialized. After Elaine and I had exchanged just a few words, she offered to have dinner another night. Jim and I seemed to be joined by electric rays, like a pair of supercharged flamenco dancers.

I stood by my plan to eat with Elaine and her husband, Andy, both of whom lived in New Orleans. They assured me that the leafy city wasn't as dangerous as I thought. As we were walking from their car to the restaurant, Elaine screamed, "What is he doing to that child?"

She bolted across the street. I glimpsed a man holding a two-year-old upside down by one leg and hitting him as hard as he could. Andy charged after Elaine to save her life, and I rushed to a pharmacy security guard.

"Please come!" I begged. "A man is killing a child!"

He followed me, and we found the man snarling at Elaine. The big security guard calmed everyone down, and we left the angry man in his hands. The man hitting the boy was drunk and said that the toddler was being bad.

I admired Elaine, who had a house full of dogs and longed for a child of her own. What courage, to risk death to save a boy from being hit. She never hesitated, and I wished that I could be as brave as she was.

To save money, I had booked a 6:30 a.m. flight, so that I had to get up at four. In the moist morning blackness, I left the key in the room and lifted my brown bag into the waiting van. Most of the way home I cried as I read, thinking of what awaited me when I returned.

"You've been crying!" yelled Diego as soon as he saw me. "You've been crying for HIM, haven't you?"

I had been weeping for what I was returning to, not for what I was leaving, but how could I tell Diego that? I said no, I wasn't crying for Jim, as we raced down the Grand Central Parkway. When we got home, I called the hotel to ask if they had found my key, and I joked with the clerk. Diego screamed that I was a whore. I had been having sex with the clerk too.

Groucho Marx

My father and I visited eleven nursing homes. Despite the horror of our mission, I loved those trips. We relished our lunches at fast-food buffets, and no one screamed at us all day.

The homes varied in their characters like the withered people within them. In some, the stench of urine brought tears to my eyes as soon as I opened the door. One resounded with squeals, since alarms went off whenever inmates rose from their chairs. What struck me most was the dearth of men—almost every soul rotting in those halls was female. They sat parked in rows, their mouths hanging open, their nostrils sucking steamy air thick with food. *Is this what awaits us?* I wondered. My father must have been asking himself that too. Women outlast men—but what kind of lives do we look forward to?

On one of these scouting trips, my father asked me how things were going with Diego. The car trembled as we paused on the rushing highway, waiting to make a left turn. Without thinking, I began to cry.

"He calls me a whore," I said.

"You'd better get a lawyer," my father answered.

In late March, a bright, clean-smelling home

announced that it had a free bed. *Someone must have died*, I thought. My father would take my mother and spend the day, then go home alone that night.

That morning, I couldn't rouse Diego. With breakfast on the table, I pulled him out of bed. Diego dawdled and cursed. I had to take him to school, then drive an hour to Adamsville, where my father sat waiting miserably. As we approached the parkway, we talked about how we might separate. I said that I wouldn't support him beyond the fall, and he went wild with rage.

"You want to know what your problem is?" he yelled.

From inside of me a voice spoke out. "You are the problem," I said.

Diego bellowed at me to stop the car, and he slammed the door so that it rocked crazily. I pulled away and nearly drove to Adamsville, but I feared what he would do if I left him by the road. I circled back and drove him to school, silent, angry, and white.

Before I reached the nursing home, I bought some rice pudding at an Adamsville strip mall. I swallowed it, sticky and creamy. It was the only food that I ate all day.

I found my father at a bare dining table, my mother crouched across from him. Her eyes shot fire like flamethrowers.

"I want to go home!" she cried.

Years of seminars and support groups had prepared my father for this moment. He said what they had told him to say:

"This is your home now."

"This is your home," she mocked, twitching with rage.

She rose on sticklike legs and advanced threateningly. "You're—you're *dumping* me here!"

She kicked him, then clawed him with her stubby nails. White foam bubbled in the corners of her mouth. She looked like the horse that pulled Scarlett to Tara, only she wouldn't flop down dead. My father's expression didn't change, but a tear slid down his cheek.

I decided someone had to be strong, so I did the only thing I could think of. Over the table's hard, reflecting surface, I talked about Groucho Marx. I filled the empty room with all the singers and manicurists who piled into the cabin until it exploded. My father laughed as he remembered the mischievous man waving dozens of people into the tiny space.

My mother never stopped raging, but she ceased kicking and clawing. A lady with dull blue eyes snagged her elbow, and they shuffled off down the corridor like two dolls on a conveyor belt. My father and I drove to our respective homes—he to guilty silence, me to something else.

Late the night before, Diego had announced that he had a paper due the next day. I had told him I would lose my job if I wrote it, but I helped him compose an outline. When I came home, I found him wild-eyed. His business teacher had thrown his draft back at him, saying she wanted a real paper, not some goddamn outline. After screaming at her, he had injured his foot kicking a newspaper machine. At the bus station, a man had attacked him with a broken bottle. I said I was sorry, but I wished that I could be more like his business teacher.

The Fish Shower Curtain

S oon after my mother entered the nursing home, I flew to a conference in Georgia. This time Diego didn't want to go. Instead, he drove Nadia to New York with his German friends and got an $80 parking ticket. We didn't find out until the second warning, since someone took the ticket off the car. Altogether it cost me $155, plus several hours on the phone.

In Georgia, I walked past redbrick buildings, raising my chin so I could drink the sun. Furtively, I breathed the sweet spring air, fearing I would get caught. The last afternoon, I sat down in the union and wrote a long letter to Jim. I knew I shouldn't write him, since his wife picked up his mail, but the letter wasn't about him and me. I was asking for help.

A student I was tutoring had taught me to use email, and I gave Jim my email address. He responded immediately with sympathetic advice, and from then on, I had the comfort of his voice. Mornings at nine Diego left me in the parking lot, and I rushed to my office to see what Jim had written. Between students, I sent out bottled messages, describing things Diego had said and done. For the first time in a year and a half, I dared to communicate with another soul. Nothing sexy or affectionate passed between us, but Diego noticed the difference right away. When we drove home, I sat like a stone as we whizzed through a tunnel of yellow forsythia. I couldn't tell Diego any of my thoughts, but they thrummed against Nadia's gray walls. *We're living in a world of beautiful flowers*, I thought, *and I'm trapped in a metal box and can't get out.*

"Say something! What are you thinking?" shouted Diego.

Our fights grew worse. Besides my silence, they focused on Germany, since to my amazement, I had won a scholarship to do research in Hamburg for three months. Diego bragged about how he was going to learn German. He would fly over early, fly over late—every day his plans changed. I dreamed of crossing the ocean without him. In my head, I had already left him; I was just figuring out how to do it. If Diego went with me to Germany, I would get nothing done. I would learn no German, do no research, and be told daily that I was a whore. I knew I was close to the breaking point and that I was capable of suicide. I couldn't bear to be called a bitch one more time.

So one day I told him. I was going to Hamburg alone. Diego exploded.

"¡Éso sí que es el colmo!" This was the limit! I was a selfish, fucking bitch.

"With you," I said calmly, "my apartment doesn't

belong to me, my body doesn't belong to me, and my life doesn't belong to me."

"¡Puta! ¡Zorra!" he screamed.

I started packing my clothes.

"What are you doing?" he yelled. "Stop that!"

My suits begged me to fold them faster. The problem was, I was starving, and it was nearly ten at night. As we fought, I made myself fish sticks and peas and shoveled them into my mouth. When I had eaten, I realized I was too tired to drive forty-five minutes to my father's house. I could have an accident and kill someone. Sick with horror, I knew I had failed. I would have to sleep with Diego another night. On my shoulder, I felt friendly bear scratches. Crying, I scratched Diego back and took him in my arms. I unpacked my clothes.

A few days later in the attic, our fight flared up again. I renewed my vow to go to Hamburg alone.

"I want to see you dead," said Diego, "and I'm going to do everything I can to ruin your life."

"¡No me hagas daño!" Don't hurt me! I squeaked. My upraised arms x-ed out my face.

Diego drank until I poured our remaining liquor down the sink. Loudly he ordered me to buy more, but I refused. As I carried my suitcase down to Nadia, he told me I was condemning him to life as a junkie. If I left, he'd be shooting up in the plaza, just like his friends from school.

"If you do, it's not my fault. It's your choice," I said.

I drove to my father's house. On the way, I bought a shower curtain at Nice-Price. If I was going to live with my father, I wanted to bring something new into the house. In the pink bathroom I had shared with my sister, the stiff shower curtain had turned black where it clung to the tub. On the new one, brilliant fish glided through glossy blue. The bathroom reeked of plastic for weeks.

My father welcomed me, relieved that I had escaped at last. But Diego didn't give up easily. We counted the number of times the phone rang. Seventeen. Eighteen. Nineteen. Finally, I answered, but it wasn't him—it was my sister. Coming from a world where things happened through networks, he had called her in California. Thrilled to see me humiliated, she shouted that she would take charge. She knew what to do! I had to go back to Diego, because he was going to kill himself.

But I didn't go back. When he threatened suicide, I told him to call the suicide hotline. I tried to survive in my parents' house. Without my mother, it wasn't so bad. And my father did a beautiful thing: when my sister announced she was leaving her husband too, he told her not to come. She hurled buckets of guilt. All our lives, our parents had favored me. Why was *I* entitled to shelter when she wasn't? I wouldn't have known how to answer that question, but my father stood firm. The thought of two tormentors joining forces to destroy me was more than he could bear. My sister would have to leave her husband another time.

With my mother gone, the house became an almost peaceful place. I had to drive an hour to campus, but I didn't care. On the days I stayed home and graded, I could work as long as I liked. Between papers, I cleaned and organized and hauled brush out of the yard. I extracted a pile of branches the size of a small house. The neighbors said they couldn't believe one person could have schlepped so much in one day.

I got reminders, though, that I wasn't in my own space. One night I came home to find Farah, a manipulative nurse who had tended my mother. Farah maintained my father as a useful acquaintance and dropped by periodically, unannounced. Wilting with fatigue, I had to wait an hour before I could eat, while she feigned sympathy about my marriage. I realized I was living in a wide-open space, since my father, not I, controlled who entered. What did women do who paid more than half their income in rent and had to flee monsters living in their space? Diego and I had both signed the lease, but only I earned enough to pay rent. I *had* to pay it, but Diego had a legal right to live there. What would I have done, where could I have gone, if it hadn't been for my father?

The telephone became an instrument of torture, a tube that dripped poison into my mind. Every night Diego called and screamed how awful I was.

"¡Eres MALA! MALA!"

I was starving him, killing him! I didn't know the meaning of love, when he had given up everything for me. One night I had been crying for an hour, holding the torture instrument to my ear. I was lying on my father's bed, my face wet and blurred, when something flickered in the doorway. My father was hovering timidly, an agonized expression on his face.

"Just hang up," he whispered. "He's tearing your guts out. Don't let him do that to you."

I didn't dare hang up, but I stopped talking to Diego soon after that.

In bursts of courage, I went on rescue missions. Spurred by my sister's report of her friend's father who had burned her mother's clothes, I raided our apartment on the way to work. Even though I knew Diego wouldn't be there, my heart pounded with terror. I loaded as much as I could into the car, carrying my French suits in my arms like Rhett lifting Scarlett. Actually, I felt more like Rambo than like Rhett.

"I'm gettin' you outa here," I muttered into the pastel mound.

My neighbor Vinny watched my progress, asking sympathetically if he could help. He held the door open as I hurled the suits in the back. Here was something that Diego wouldn't burn.

On campus, though, I couldn't avoid him, and he attacked at will. At any time, he might appear in my office. He struck me like a fist that came from a different direction each time. No sooner had I recovered from a punch in the nose when the next one caught me on the ear. One day he appeared, demanding money.

"Give me 7,500 dollars," he ordered, "and I'll sign the fucking separation agreement."

The next day he came back to say, "I'm not signing a fucking thing."

Diego had gotten the $7,500 figure from the time I'd estimated my net worth for renter's insurance. Carefully, I had assessed my Korean appliances and my hand-finished furniture. He was entitled to half of everything I owned! He knew his rights! My lawyer, who had drawn up the separation agreement, said that I would have to pay him alimony. I questioned the justice of this. Shouldn't he have to pay back everything he'd sucked out of me? At the same time, I knew that it worked to my advantage to be a woman. How would some guy look if he dumped his foreign wife because she was chronically angry?

Diego used all of his wits to punish me, always with the network approach. He went to my department chair and asked to enroll in my classes. As a student, he said, it was his right.

"This is so embarrassing," moaned the chair.

Then Diego started coming to my classes. He would stick his head in the door and grin.

"If you don't go away, I'll call security," I said.

"You've got to share," urged a shocked student.

I figured my students deserved an explanation, so I said, "Make sure not to marry anyone unless you know him really well."

I shed no tears even when he came to my night class, more frightening since the campus was half-deserted. I asked my students to close the door, and when the class ended, to wait with me until a security guard could walk me to my car. The two most fawning volunteered to stay, but I felt grateful for their bulky male bodies.

"You look like you've seen a ghost!" exclaimed a woman who commuted from Staten Island.

"Some people don't know when to say when," said one of the protective guys.

The worst materialization of the poltergeist came when I was teaching Thomas Mann to my honors students. Diego popped in the door and yelled, "¡Hay una PUTA por aquí!" There's a BITCH around here!

Each time he accosted me, I walked grimly to the security office and filed a report. They knew Diego well, since he had been causing trouble all over campus. My university was run by hardworking women, and he treated them as he treated me. He wanted to talk to them with their office doors closed. He threatened his female teachers, yelling about his rights. With shame I realized it was all my fault. I had brought this monster into the country. I had escaped him, but my university and government were paying the price. I had touched off an avalanche but had sidestepped the flow.

Diego told me that if he could continue to have reduced tuition, he would sign the separation agreement. We met at a bank and had a tense, eerie exchange with a notary public who savored each detail of his oath and stamp.

"You're being very careful about this," I said.

"This is a very important document. I should be careful," he admonished.

To my amazement, Diego signed the agreement.

"He *signed* it?" asked my lawyer.

I paid the rent through the end of the summer, more

for old Fred than for Diego. But I told Diego that after August 31, he would have to find another place to live. He seemed amenable, probably thinking he could wear me down later on.

When his grandmother died in May, he demanded a ticket to Spain. With my last $500, I bought him a one-way trip. He would fly back to New York on his own and live in our apartment while I worked in Hamburg.

"No funny business. You mail me that key like you said you would," he commanded.

Here I made a mistake. Diego did fly home to his mother, and for a few weeks, I moved back into Fred's house. I cleaned up the food I had bought for Diego, which had rotted in the refrigerator. I swept up the ashes he had left in the bathtub. I even planted flowers, a crazy move since I was leaving for Hamburg in two weeks. I should have packed up everything he owned, shipped it to Spain, and changed the lock—that was Fred's idea. But I feared the consequences, and it seemed dishonorable. It would mean a double cross, a denial of everything I had promised. I didn't want to substantiate Diego's opinion of me.

My first week in Hamburg, I cried all the time. I thought I was the worst person in the world. In June, the temperature cowered around forty, and after paying my rent, I had eight dollars a day for food. But as the air warmed, I walked out into the city. In the evenings, I sat on my balcony and read *Bleak House* and *Liaisons dangereuses*. The golden light lasted until after ten, and swallows swirled in the glow behind the Nikolaikirche.

Laura Otis

I feared I would jump off my seventh-floor balcony, but I never did. I had discovered a sound that I loved. Each night the bolt snapped shut in my door. I was alone, and no one could hurt me.

Rain

I've never known it to rain as hard as it did when I was with Diego. The air roared with the sound of it, and drops bounced off the resisting roofs. Diego marveled at its force.

"¡Hostia!" he exclaimed as drops hammered our car.

It rained the day we drove to meet the real estate agent who would show us Fred's pea-green house. Even with the wipers flashing, we could barely see through the windshield. Someone seemed to be hurling buckets of water onto the car.

On Clam Cove Road, Diego thought a man had cut him off, and he took off after him, vowing to fight. His father would never tolerate such a thing! He would force him off the road and teach him to drive! With the rain roaring, I pleaded with him not to attack. Diego bellowed and cursed. The man escaped because he reached the left-hand lane, not because of anything I said.

We had an hour before our appointment, so we ate at the Walsh Avenue pancake house. My turkey-broccoli crepes stuck in my chest and broiled. A little while later, we found the agency dark and lifeless. On our answering machine, the agent had left a message too late, telling us not to come.

It rained harder the day I went to the police. When Diego popped in the back door of my night class, grinning crazily, the security guards who took my report said I'd have to go to the local police. Grim and zombielike, I went to the precinct. I found a parking space, bought a container of skim milk at a bodega to get change, and dropped fifty cents in the meter. My umbrella bent under the force of the water. I had to tilt it to keep my head dry, and by the time I reached the police station, my legs were soaked. I walked into an inner-city precinct where gang members, drug dealers, and junkies slouched. I managed not to cry as I told the sympathetic officers why I had come. They said there was nothing they could do; I needed to file a protection order.

"My lawyer says I can only get one if he hits me," I explained.

Subtly, they suggested I exaggerate a little. I should say whatever it took to get him away from me. Thinking of the fifty cents I had lost, I walked slowly back to Nadia. I didn't think I could do it. If I lied, I'd be doing an injustice to all the women who do get hit.

It rained hardest the morning I went to see my lawyer. Diego was due to fly to Spain that night. It was May 11, the crux of final exam week, when every second counted. The night before, I had driven back to our apartment to spend the night with Diego. My father had begged me not to go, certain that Diego was going to kill me. He had agreed to go home to Spain on the condition I spend one last night with him. Diego always had conditions, and I wanted to honor my part of the bargain. With my stomach turning, I sucked him until he came, purely in the interest of sleep. It didn't work. He kept me up crying and accusing all night, and by morning I was a jangling wreck.

To reach the lawyer, I had to drive an hour and a half in pounding rain. With my nose to the windshield, I could barely see ten feet in front of me. I reached the lawyer's office and found no one there. With the rain roaring, I drove to a doughnut shop, alongside of which stood a phone booth. The rain beat on that booth like a hundred men with rubber mallets, so that it might shatter any moment. I called the lawyer's office and got no answer, then called Diego to see if he had left a message. The lawyer had left no word, but Diego had lost his passport.

That was it. I couldn't take any more. As rain hammered the booth, I howled with pain. Water spouted from me so that I choked and couldn't see. I wished that someone would find me and ask what was wrong, but no one came. In that streaming cell, I cried all alone. The one-way ticket to Spain was my last hope. I had paid my last $500 for it and had no money left. Without his passport, Diego couldn't fly, and then how would I get rid of him? My father was right: Diego was going to kill me, but not with one quick, angry blow.

I decided to drive an hour back to campus, and on impulse, I stopped at the lawyer's office. This time he was there, and he did his best to hearten me. After I drove back, I took Diego to the airport. He had found his passport, and the rain was lightening.

Those hours together at JFK tore up my insides. Diego left his backpack at security, and we raced across the terminal to recover it. Haggard and wild-eyed, we panted with fear and rage. I was surprised no one tried to stop us. Nowadays we would both have been detained as a pair of inept terrorists.

Diego vowed he wouldn't get on the plane. I was going to screw him over. I would abandon him. I promised him more and more: continued tuition benefits, help with rent, anything to keep him away. My life had become a great bleeding wound, and as my father said, I should give priority to stopping the bleeding. Diego was a dull ax hacking at me, and he had to be restrained. If he didn't get on the plane, I would sprint for Nadia and leave him at JFK. I pictured social services hunting me down when he was picked up raving in the terminal. I didn't care what they did to him. I would say that he'd attacked me.

With a sad, uncertain wave, Diego disappeared through the gate.

"He got on the plane?" asked my father.

"Yes," I answered.

I never figured out why.

The Leather Glove

When I reached Hamburg, I told Fred I was moving. That gave him three months to find a new tenant. Diego flew back to New York and reclaimed the apartment, but he knew he had to be out by September 1.

When I did come home—to my father's house—I heard from Fred. His new tenant had balked at the last minute. Did I still want the place? Now, here was a risk. If I said yes and Diego wouldn't leave, I'd be homeless and lose half my salary for a year. But I liked living at Fred's place, and moving was expensive. I took a chance and stayed, and Diego kept his word. By the time classes started, he had moved to a friend's garage in Belle Meade. Fred and his wife, Teresa, urged me to change the locks.

Ever since I had moved to Fred's pea-green house, I had dreamed that all the space was mine. Elated, I bought bookcases, a peach quilt, and a great big Sony TV. I tore the covers off pillows and scrubbed away Diego's sweat; I yanked up dead flowers he hadn't watered and planted pink and white chrysanthemums. With violent energy, I fought to restore stunted life.

Unfortunately, communications continued. On

campus I encountered Diego almost each day. He didn't call often, but when he did, I made a mistake. I told him I was going to visit Javi in Baltimore.

Diego had always suspected that I wanted to have sex with Javi. While home alone, Diego had read the Spanish parts of my diary, the only pages he could understand. There I had written of a siesta in Granada that had involved some good-natured groping. Javi and I had stopped short of sex, but to Diego, it was all the same.

Like Diego, Javi had come to America with a woman. At the time, he could barely speak English. He had worked as a busboy and had become a professor because he studied like a demon, treated people well, and fearlessly pursued opportunities. In the beginning, Javi had offered Diego advice, but Diego saw him as a nemesis.

When the semester started, I did a wicked thing. Since I would be up for tenure soon, I wanted to make sure I wasn't abusing my college. I called the benefits office. Could a legally separated spouse still receive half-price tuition? Of course, they said no. It saved them $3,000 a semester, and I became a villain who had gone back on her word. Diego declared war, and the hostilities escalated. He came to my office to threaten me, and he frightened the other professors.

Once while I was talking on the phone to my team-teaching partner, he bellowed and pounded on my office door. The office had no windows, no means of escape. I watched the heavy wooden door shake and wondered if it was going to hold.

"What's all that noise?" demanded my partner.

I said it was my angry ex-husband. She told me to hang up and call the police, so I cut her off and called security. By the time they got there, Diego was gone, and I felt ashamed and silly.

Another afternoon he came to curse me, and I shouted that he was a parasite sucking my blood. It happened in Spanish, and I gambled that no one nearby would understand. After Diego left, the big, handsome Russian teacher came in from across the hall. Was I all right? he asked. I felt as though I'd been spewing sewage into his office. I said how sorry I was that he had had to hear all that. He said he didn't care, as long as I was safe. He was seeing a woman who had just been through an excruciating divorce.

Diego and I met face-to-face in a crowded hallway of the student union. The fall had turned cold, and I was shivering in my brown coat with a fur collar. Diego stalked up to me and stuck his face in mine.

"Are you going to see Javi? You can't do that! How can you do that?" he spat.

Diego's face was white with fury. I said I wasn't going to have sex with Javi. I just wanted to talk to him. A river of students flowed around the snag that we were creating. Diego forbade me to visit Javi, and I said that I was going. He was wearing heavy leather gloves, and he hurled one down in front of me with a smack. Was he challenging me to a duel? I prayed that none of the passing students were mine.

The next day Diego's mother called me. How could I do this to him? If you're with a Spaniard, you can't just go visit another "chico." To her I was still sixteen. I told her we were legally separated, and I could do as I liked. She thought I was deliberately provoking him.

"He may have insulted you, but you have to stand by him," she insisted. "In Spain, you'd be obligated, OBLIGADA, to support him."

Insulted? It seemed insane for anyone to use that word for what I'd been hearing. I said he had taken two years of my life, and I didn't owe him anything.

Diego kept the situation so critical that I never went to see Javi. Each day he set off a new explosion. Late one afternoon he pounded on my apartment door, demanding his nightstand and computer files. I refused to let him in, fearing that he might kill me, and yelled back at him through the locked door. He mocked my Spanish, trying to make me lose control. He knew what infuriated me most.

"Oh my *gawd*," I heard Carol saying.

In their living room though the flimsy wall, she and Ted could hear each ugly word. I pitied and feared them as I hustled the heavy nightstand down the stairs. How they must have despised us! Frantically, I transferred Diego's files to a disk, but the computer crashed. I said I'd have to give them to him another time. Diego threatened, bellowed, and cursed.

"I'm not leaving without my fucking files! I know my rights! Open the fucking door!"

I wouldn't, and he rattled and kicked it furiously. He demanded an immediate divorce. I said that was fine, and I called my lawyer.

"He wants a divorce now?" he asked.

Diego hadn't wanted a divorce last spring, because of the tuition reduction and his green card. I had opted for the separation agreement, though my father had urged me to get divorced. Now I was all too happy to file, and my lawyer was glad to prepare the papers. The suit cost me $300. The process server had trouble finding Diego, although I supplied his home address and all his workplaces. The server finally caught him at 7:30 a.m. Horrified, Diego called me, then came to my office.

"¡Saca la denuncia!" Withdraw the suit, he demanded.

I wouldn't.

On alternate days he roared and threatened, or groveled and begged. I never knew which Diego I would get. Once he appeared with the lease and his immigration papers, loudly reading phrases he marked with his finger. On other days, his feigned subjection seemed oddly familiar, and I remembered where I had seen it. In a Hamburg subway station, I had asked a Roma woman if I had the right track, and she had assumed a staged posture of begging. Her cringing was so contrived that I gave her nothing even though she'd given me directions. How could she expect me to respond to that false look? Diego affected me the same way.

When I wouldn't withdraw the suit, he went to my colleagues and showed them the divorce papers.

"Do you have to do this?" I asked. "I'm up for tenure soon."

"Saca la denuncia, and they'll see you're a good person, and then you'll get tenure," he said.

I wouldn't. Outraged, he refused to relent.

Finally, I went to the vice provost, the scariest woman I had ever met. At our orientation, she had said we could come to her if we had a problem with sexual harassment. Trembling, I explained my situation and said how sorry I was. She looked at me for a long time with eyes that swirled like barbed chariot wheels.

"We can keep him from taking your classes. We can do that," she said.

I replied that I was grateful.

"But how are you going to get rid of him?" she asked.

"I don't know," I said.

The General Comes

W hen Diego told me his mother was coming, I burst into tears. It was late November, a time when every minute counted, and I had so many papers to grade that five hours of sleep were a luxury. Diego yelled at me that I had to go, since they were flying from Spain to talk about the breakup. After all, she was giving me three days' notice!

My father grew worried when he heard there'd be two of them—the mother and Rosario, who liked to take charge.

"Let me come with you," he begged.

But I pictured it, and it seemed absurd—him with no Spanish, them with no English, and me in the middle, translating for my inquisitors and a frightened old man. Somehow, I would have to do it alone.

In the late afternoons, trains ran every two hours, so that I could arrive an hour and a half early or ten minutes late. I took the later train and burned up Seventh Avenue to their hotel, trusting my legs more than a cab.

My father would have been relieved, since the two

silver-blonde Spaniards didn't kidnap, drug, or berate me. They didn't even try to melt me with guilt. Instead, they talked about donus. Un donus, a round, sugary food with a religious sound. They confessed that for dinner last night, they had eaten two donus apiece. If they kept this up, they'd be as fat as the Americans, who scandalized them with their size. Not likely, I said. Don't worry. The gordos ate a dozen donus at a time.

For dinner they ordered chicken breasts and chewed them silently. Their tucked-in elbows and expert grips on their knives advertised their social class. While they swallowed, I told them the break with Diego was final, but I emphasized his ability to survive. He had been delivering flowers and the week before had left sweet white roses hanging in plastic on my front door.

"What a nice gesture!" exclaimed María del Rosario.

The falseness of her expression frightened me. Like Diego, she had a contrived look, geared to stir a certain response. It scared me that she thought I could be so unseeing. She and Diego imagined me as reacting, the way a tree drops nuts if you shake a branch.

I had dumped Diego's flowers on the compost heap after unpeeling the plastic to recycle. I didn't tell that to Rosario. It was enough to know it, to see it inside.

The one eruption came when Rosario paid for dinner. Living with her mother, she kept all her earnings and spent them on meals and tailored clothes. As we were leaving, the waitress followed her out to say she hadn't left enough tip.

The next day, Diego called me with a sneer in his

voice. He had heard I'd arrived half an hour late. The General and her daughter had studied me and found me determined. They were over the Atlantic Ocean on their way back to Spain.

Voices

No matter which way I walk through my mind, I exit a cell and find Diego. The only way not to think of him is not to think, which I try to do in my room full of stuffed animals. Still he turns up—he always does. He might be down on the street right now, his finger poised over my bell.

Last year he emailed to say he was back in law school and collecting fees in a parking lot. Rosario paid his rent so that he no longer had to live with his mother. Wouldn't I like to stop by for a coffee? When I didn't answer, he called my office and said he was a professor from Murcia. I knew his voice right away, bizarre English taut with rage.

"This is Professor Reyes of Murcia!" he yelled over what sounded like the roar of a bar. "I just want to know. One week ago, I have send you an email. I want to know did you receive it!"

"No, I'm sorry, I didn't receive it," I said, on the chance it really was Professor Reyes. "Why don't you send it again?"

"Yes, that is what I will do. I will send it again!" His voice pulsed with sarcasm.

"All right, thank you," I said and hung up.

Diego won't ever go away. He will not let me rest. As long as he lives, he'll be watching, waiting to hurt me any way he can.

People developed memory for protection, but I need protection from memory. In any chamber of my mind, an open portal leads to Diego. I could seal the doors, but new ones appear. When I turn him to words, I don't purge him: I clone him.

Since no confining will keep him quiet, I must learn to live with that voice.

"¡Puta!" A wedding ring bounces off my forehead. Diego grabs Bernardo the Bear. Then he has me, scratching my back, demanding a reconciliation.

Do we all live this way? Are we stung by creatures in the cells of our minds?

If Diego died, I would feel much safer, and I think hopefully of his failing liver. But that wouldn't silence my mind's replicas of him. In me, he'll live as long as I do.

If there's hope, it lies in listening to new voices. I draw a breath and turn my mind's ear outward, to cheeping sparrows and a humming plane.

Acknowledgments

I originally wrote *The Memory Hive* as a hypertext where links at the end of each episode led to related stories. I tried to structure the hypertext the way memory works, with multiple, sometimes surprising connections between episodes. I have always been fascinated by how memories lead to one another: circling, spiraling, leaping unexpectedly, doing anything but progressing. I wanted to write a story with as many possibilities as a remembering mind. When I published *The Memory Hive* as a novel, however, I decided to remove the links because they were distracting readers from the story. The episodes themselves were already moving in a nonlinear way.

For the hive image, I am indebted to Jorge Luis Borges, whose story "La biblioteca de Babel" ("The Library of Babel") invites readers to imagine the infinite possibilities of hexagonal spaces. *The Memory Hive* does not draw on and is not related to any websites, software, or other fiction with the same name.

The Memory Hive refers to the following creative works:

Almodóvar, Pablo, director. *Entre tinieblas*. Produced by Luis Calvo. Tesauro. 1983.

Borges, Jorge Luis. "La biblioteca de Babel." *Ficciones*. Alianza Editorial. 1985 [1941].

Cervantes, Miguel de. *Don Quijote de La Mancha*. Edited by Martín de Riquer. 9th edition. 2 volumes. Editorial Juventud. 1979 [1605–1615].

Donaldson, Roger, director. *Cocktail*. Produced by Ted Field and Robert W. Cort. Buena Vista Pictures. 1988.

Fein, Bernard, and Albert S. Ruddy, creators. *Hogan's Heroes*. Produced by Edward H. Feldman. CBS Television. 1965–1971.

Flaubert, Gustave. *Madame Bovary*. Éditions Gallimard. 1972 [1857].

Fleming, Victor, director. *Gone with the Wind*. Produced by David O. Selznick. Selznick International Pictures. Loew's Inc. 1939.

Hanna, William, and Joseph Barbera, creators, directors, and producers. *The Flintstones*. ABC Television. 1960–1966.

Hill, George Roy, director. *The World According to Garp*. Produced by George Roy Hill. Warner Bros. 1982.

Kotcheff, Ted, director. *First Blood*. Produced by Buzz Feitshans. Anabasis Investments, N. V. Orion Pictures. 1982.

Lyne, Adrian, director. *Fatal Attraction*. Produced by Stanley R. Jaffe and Sherry Lansing. Paramount Pictures. 1987.

Mankiewicz, Joseph L., director. *Guys and Dolls*. Produced by Samuel Goldwyn. Metro-Goldwyn-Mayer. 1955.

Morgan, Carey, and Lee David. "The Other Day I Met a Bear." Traditional American camp song. 1919.

Newell, Mike, director. *Four Weddings and a Funeral*. Produced by Duncan Kenworthy. PolyGram Filmed Entertainment, Channel Four Films, and Working Title Films. 1994.

Pakula, Alan J., director. *The Pelican Brief*. Based on *The Pelican Brief* by John Grisham. Warner Bros. 1993.

Parton, Dolly. "I Will Always Love You." Performed by Whitney Houston. *The Bodyguard*. Produced by David Foster. Arista Label. 1992.

The Police. *Synchronicity*. Produced by the Police and Hugh Padgham. A&M Label. 1983.

Pynchon, Thomas. *Gravity's Rainbow*. Viking Press. 1973.

Revaux, Jacques, composer, and Paul Anka, lyricist. "My Way." Performed by Frank Sinatra. Produced by Sonny Burke. Reprise Label. 1969.

Roddenberry, Gene, creator. *Star Trek: The Original Series*. Desilu Productions. Paramount Domestic Television. 1966–1969.

Verhoeven, Paul, director. *Basic Instinct*. Produced by Alan Marshall. TriStar Pictures. 1992.

Wolfe, Tom. *The Bonfire of the Vanities*. Farrar, Strauss, Giroux. 1987.

Wood, Sam, director. *A Night at the Opera*. Produced by Irving Thalberg. Metro-Goldwyn-Mayer. 1935.

Wyler, William, director. *Mrs. Miniver*. Produced by Sidney Franklin. Loew's Inc. 1942.

Yerkovich, Anthony, creator. *Miami Vice*. Produced by Michael Mann and Anthony Yerkovich. NBCUniversal Television. 1984–1990.

Printed in the United States
By Bookmasters